Where True Beauty Lies:

A Modernization of the Book of Esther

Patty Lesser

To Roni
Lots of love
Patty

CAVERN
OF DREAMS
PUBLISHING

Where True Beauty Lies: A Modernization of the Book of Esther

Author's Note: This is a work of fiction. Names, characters, places, and incidents are a product of the author's imagination. Locales and public names are sometimes used for atmospheric purposes. Any resemblance to actual people, living or dead, or to businesses, companies, events, institutions, or locales is entirely coincidental.

Ordering Information:
Books may be ordered directly through the publisher, **Cavern of Dreams Publishing**
info@cavernofdreams.com
www.cavernofdreams.com
Discounts are available for volume orders.

ISBN: 978-1-989027-01-1 (softcover)

Also available by the author on Amazon:

The Perfect Hand

Devouring Time

A Discerning Heart

That Truthful Place

Locker Rooms

Shall We Chat?
Revealing the Secrets of Chatting Online

For Liz Kyle, RIP

It was at your funeral I was inspired
to write this story.

Chapter One

Tonight, in Europe, the tiny country of Baltia held its most prestigious gala of the year. Famous and influential people from all over the world put their lives on hold to travel to Baltia to honour its auspicious president, Thomas Edmonds. He had just succeeded in accomplishing a great feat for his country.

Baltia now boasted a sound and increasing economic base, allowing its people a comfortable lifestyle. No one suffered from poverty. The world had appeared at the party to learn the president's secrets. They hoped to learn how he had triumphed where they had failed.

This evening's grand affair showed off youth and beauty. The extravagant dresses worn by the women had been created solely for this event. Notable designers used fabrics such as silk, velvet, satin, and taffeta; most were off-the-shoulder, full-skirted gowns reaching the floor. Jewellery glittered all over the room. The women enjoyed showing off their wealth.

The men were equally resplendent in black tuxedos with a variety of bright handkerchiefs in their front jacket pockets to match their silk ties. The fusion of colours arrayed in the massive ballroom resembled a packed garden of flowers.

Though the president and the first lady arrived together, the pair quickly parted upon entering the ballroom. The president grabbed the first waiter he saw and removed a drink from his tray before heading towards the group of serious men to his right. His stunning wife made her way over to the flashy women chattering happily to the left.

Everyone's eyes rested on the president as he glided across the floor. Every man envied him, and every woman wished she were married to him.

Baltia's citizens named Thomas "The People's President," because he always made himself available to speak to anyone about any problem they had. His people loved him and declared he was the best president ever.

Thomas Edmonds has held the position of president for ten years now. No one remembered the beginning of his presidency when he had made a few mistakes and everything was a little shaky. As the years progressed, the president improved their lives by providing everyone with a job, and the people couldn't be happier.

Baltia's president was a complicated and controlled man, yet he was very charismatic. His mathematical mind worked out any difficulty he encountered. He loved to charm people and impress them with his bright personality.

Thomas was a man of impressive height at six-foot-three. He kept his slightly greying hair well-groomed. Tonight, he boasted a tuxedo created by Baltia's top male designer. He wore a delightful blue silk tie that matched the blue silk handkerchief in his breast pocket. His deep, ocean-blue eyes matched his outfit and took in everything going on around him.

Growing up, Thomas was closely tied to his younger brother, Martin. The brothers did everything together. Both excelled as students and prospered on the soccer field. As soon as they became teenagers, their illustrious father began to groom them in the world of politics. Both parents believed that was a noble profession for their sons.

The young men started at the bottom in lower political positions, but they soon moved up the ladder. In their late twenties, they were elected to the posts of mayor (Thomas) and assistant mayor (Martin) of Graton. Because they worked so well together, the city rose to great heights.

Thomas had completed three terms as mayor when the position of president became vacant. He applied for the opportunity to lead the country, and an election was held. Thomas won by the narrowest of margins; some thought he was a little young for the job. When he was elected president, his brother assumed the role of Graton's mayor.

Between the two of them, they ruled over the small country with brilliant success, changing it into one of the best places in the world to live. Unfortunately, their father died two months after Thomas was named president, but at least he saw his son reach that great position.

Thomas's chief concern was poverty, and he worked very hard to abolish it. It hurt him to see people struggle and suffer. With the assistance of all the mayors and the heads of every major company, Thomas found a job for every able person. This required much time to achieve, but when the plan was completed, Baltia became a prosperous country.

Everyone's talents had been put to use in creating a better environment. No family suffered from lack of food for their table. As the wealth of the country increased, crime went down, and the country remained at peace.

At the gala, the president was constantly being interrupted by important and illustrious people who begged an audience. People crowded around him, and he would see to it that he spoke with everyone.

Austria's president stepped forward and offered Thomas his right hand. "It's a pleasure to see you again."

"The pleasure is all mine," said Thomas, shaking the offered hand. A genuine open smile played on his lips. "Have you resolved that issue concerning your immigration policies?"

"Yes, thanks to your advice." The Austrian president grinned. "I appreciate your time and effort."

"Any time, my friend, any time." Thomas waved to the waiter. He dropped his empty glass on his tray and picked up another tempting concoction.

A regal woman in an ornate, golden gown reached over to Thomas and placed her hand on his arm. He turned his attention to her.

The queen of Denmark said, "We're fascinated with what you've accomplished here."

Thomas smiled, but his cheeks were a little red. "I'd be pleased to help in any way possible."

"How do you encourage people to work?" asked the American president, getting down to business. The USA, as well as other countries, had problems with its welfare system.

The group leaned in, waiting expectantly for Thomas's response.

Brushing back some dark hairs that had fallen across his face, Thomas made a point to glance into everyone's eyes, but it was a little hard to focus. "When people obtain the opportunity to experience a fulfilling day, they encourage themselves. Do what you love, and you'll never work another day."

"How did you create so many jobs?" asked the king of Belgium, gesturing with a glass of champagne in his hand.

Thomas placed his right hand on the man's shoulder to steady himself and said, "Delegate."

The American president appeared surprised. "So everyone is working for someone else?"

Thomas bowed to the man and said, "Yes."

"What if the position is unsuitable?" asked the queen of Denmark. Her exquisite gown showed off her bare, white shoulders.

Thomas turned towards her. "Everyone has a three-month probation period. During that time, they are evaluated and each person can decide what's best for them."

"What if it isn't?" asked the king of Belgium. He didn't seem to believe this could be successful.

"Then they are given the opportunity to try something else."

Everyone nodded thoughtfully.

"How are their salaries decided?" asked the Brazilian president. He placed his empty glass on the platter held by a waiter and picked up a glass of champagne.

"Everyone is paid equally," replied Thomas. He tried to stand straight to emphasize the point.

"Isn't that unfair?" asked the American president, puffing out his chest. "Why should a doctor receive the same salary as a street cleaner?"

"My people accept that every job has its own importance. All disciplines require hard work." Thomas's eyes darted around. His eye fell on the nearest waiter. With a wink, he placed his glass on the tray and grabbed another.

The king of Belgium cleared his throat as everyone watched Thomas's actions. "How much is everyone paid?"

"80,000 Euros a year," Thomas stated, holding in a burp.

"How can you afford to do that?" asked the startled queen of Denmark.

"The accumulated money enters the financial branch of our government. We pay each citizen's salary."

"And the people accept that?" enquired the American president. He played with the wedding ring on his finger.

"Yes," Thomas affirmed. He revealed a couple of wrinkles around his eyes when he squinted. "Now the people are self-sufficient. No one goes hungry in Baltia, and crime is non-existent."

"Brilliant," gushed the king of Denmark, holding up his glass in salute. "But how did you decide on the amount?"

"We reviewed our economics, the cost of living, and personal value. We decided 80,000 should suffice. We can provide you with our financial reports allowing you to judge for yourselves."

More notable personages entered Thomas's circle and asked more pertinent questions. With straight and honest answers, he tried to reply to everyone as best as he could.

After a short lull in the conversation, Thomas glanced across the room. He noticed his pretty wife in deep discussion with her shallow, arrogant friends who believed Leah's life was perfect, and they were all envious.

Leah Edmonds was elegantly dressed in an original, tight black ball gown designed by Marcus Wolf, the top designer in Baltia. A long slit down her right side showed off a sculpted leg. Her naturally blonde hair was masterfully arranged in soft curls around her face.

She wore her most expensive jewellery for this exclusive event. A diamond tiara with ten perfectly round diamonds crowned her head. On her fingers, she wore two brilliant diamond rings made with platinum. Her diamond earrings were 18k rose gold with rose-cut diamonds.

To Leah, it was of the utmost importance she dress better and more richly than anyone else in the room. Hours were required to prepare for this event. She had hired a hairdresser, a makeup artist, and a dresser to prepare her gown.

Growing up in New York City, Leah (nee Rosewood) had a privileged childhood. Her father was an important man in politics, and her mother spent much of her time with her many charities. Though they provided her with everything, both parents had little time for their awkward, silly daughter who didn't have much intelligence.

The only quality time the child had with her mother was in the evenings when she dressed for one of her many social events. Leah craved those few moments with her mother, where she learned the art of being elegantly dressed.

Leah's mother felt it was important to at least install in her daughter the knowledge of looking better than everyone else. Leah was schooled in makeup, jewellery, and matching the proper accessories. It was of the utmost importance to choose the right dress for one's body, as if choosing the best wine to drink with a meal.

To Leah, her mother was an angel, and she did nothing but bathe in her bright, white light whenever she could. During the numerous luncheon meetings at their home, Leah would sneak into a hiding place behind the curtains along the far window. She absorbed her mother's appearance and those of the other well-dressed, aristocratic ladies. She would mimic their daintiness while drinking tea and eating the exquisitely cut sandwiches.

However, Leah was unable to ascertain much of their intelligent discourse, so she only absorbed the fake appearances without retaining any of the intellectual matters discussed by the women. As she grew up, she became a selfish, egotistical woman. Beneath her callousness, nothing existed.

After Leah passed through adolescence, her appearance greatly improved; she became something of a classic beauty with a thin, feminine figure. Her blue eyes shone brightly, and her facial features resembled those of a supermodel.

When Leah was in her early twenties, she met Thomas at a political function in New York City. Thomas was completely mesmerized by Leah's beauty and enjoyed having her expert social graces to assist his rise in politics. Her perfect etiquette only enhanced their social position.

The obvious leader of the rich and elegant women at the ball, Leah initiated the gossip, which only delighted the women who encircled her. While their husbands were changing the world, these women were only interested in the latest scandals.

"Did you hear about Connie?" announced Leah.

"No," replied the group.

"What has she done now?" pressed a good-looking woman in a tight green dress. Her hands fluttered in the air.

"She had a breast enhancement." Leah smiled brightly, hoping to thrill the women.

"They were big already," exclaimed a woman in a low-cut blue dress. She showed off her large and shapely breasts, but hers were real.

"How much plastic surgery has she had now?" asked a woman in a flowing yellow gown.

"Not enough." Leah grinned, loving her own joke.

"Did you hear Jeff is taking his third wife on a world cruise? He might as well. No one will accept that woman," stated the woman in the blue dress.

"Have you met her? I have. She's quite young," another woman added.

"How young is she?" Leah asked as she brought her fingers up to her lips.

"In her early thirties," answered the woman in the tight red dress.

"Thirties? How old is Jeff now? Isn't he in his seventies?" enquired the woman in the yellow taffeta.

"At least seventy," said the woman in the exquisite red dress.

"Cradle robber." Leah laughed.

The women giggled.

From the opposite end of the massive ballroom, Thomas watched as his silly but gorgeous wife revelled in her natural element. He noticed how the attractive women politely laughed at her last statement. Leah was very good at sustaining attention.

Thomas enjoyed his wife's success with people. She was always the centre of attention with everyone hanging onto her every word. However, he had realized quite suddenly a few months ago he was no longer in love with her. What he felt now was companionship out of necessity.

Shaking off those thoughts, he returned to his adoring fans. Thomas smiled and joked with them all. It was a wonderful night; the liquor flowed, and much was accomplished.

Chapter Two

At precisely nine o'clock, the full orchestra played Baltia's ceremonial waltz. Thomas, hearing the music, gazed beyond the group of important people to his wife at the other end of the room. After he finished the alcohol in his glass, he glided across the room's expanse to reach his wife's side. The women around her stood silent, taking in the president's athletic physique.

Like a conductor preparing an orchestra, Thomas lifted his right hand and held it before his wife. Leah elegantly raised her left hand and placed it in her husband's. With his other hand, he encircled her tiny waist and led her to the centre of the room.

People moved back and the dance floor was cleared. Thomas and Leah waltzed into the vacant area. All eyes were upon their attractive frames. Everyone savoured the regal beauty of their flowing motion as they elegantly danced to the melodious music.

With some skill, Thomas kept his back erect and expertly twirled his wife around the floor. He knew he cut a fine figure and he enjoyed showing off. He loved the adoration, but it was just a means to an end. He hoped these influential people would follow his success and return home to implement his laws.

When the music ended, everyone clapped. Thomas and Leah slid apart, and he held out his hand to the queen of England. She happily followed him onto the dance floor. Leah picked out the king of Croatia, who was probably the second most attractive man in the room.

As the couples danced around the room, they talked quietly to their partners. The king of Croatia commented on Leah's lovely appearance and her gorgeous gown. He showered her with compliments of which she drew immense pleasure. Her face took on a youthful glow and her lips parted as he spun her around.

Thomas and the queen were having a more serious discussion as he slowly but elegantly led her about the room.

"Would you agree to mentor my son?" England's queen asked as she locked her eyes on his. "He's a bright young man. It would be wonderful if you could groom him for his future position."

Thomas charmed her with his wide, beaming smile. "He'd be most welcome."

"You're very kind. What he could learn from you would only benefit England." The queen allowed herself to be swept up in the music.

"I'm pleased to help. If the world would only adopt my country's policies, it would be a much happier and more peaceful place."

The music ended and another waltz was played, this one from Austria. Leah smiled at her partner who bowed and passed her on to the king of Austria.

"You look as lovely as ever, my dear," said the king, who had a good relationship with Baltia's president and first lady. He had attended school with Thomas, and they had remained good friends throughout the years.

"Thank you, Stefan. If you're pleased, I'm happy," Leah said as she smiled seductively.

Stefan smiled back. "Is that a new hairstyle?"

"Yes." Leah reached up and adjusted the curls. "Do you like it?"

"It frames your face so exquisitely." Stefan pulled her tighter, and Leah sank into his body. They moved slowly around the dance floor.

Other couples soon joined in the dancing until most of the room was involved. It was truly a spectacular scene with the dresses flowing and the men standing straight and proud. Everyone enjoyed themselves.

After dutifully dancing with all the queens and first ladies, Thomas bowed to his last partner and left the dance floor. He grabbed the first waiter and picked up a glass from his tray. He held up his hand to the man as he gulped the drink down, then he placed the empty glass on the tray and removed another. After a quick sip, he walked towards a group of men standing around the food table.

Different roast and grilled meats, baked and broiled fish, a large variety of vegetables steamed and roasted, and every type of salad, lay on large plates and in bowls. At the other end of the table were delightful finger foods for those who preferred something smaller.

The men picked up plates and filled them with everything they wished. Once their plates were full, they selected cutlery. Several round tables were set up along one wall where people could sit and eat.

With his elbow, Thomas pointed to an empty table near the window. The five men placed themselves around it.

The president of Brazil spoke first. "I understand Baltia is free of crime. How can that be?" Crime was a serious problem in his country.

Though his hands shook from the amount of alcohol he had consumed, Thomas carefully placed his knife and fork on his plate. He turned towards the man on his right. "Criminals find earning an honest living is more beneficial than the stress of committing a crime."

"How did you convince them to work?" enquired the president of Haiti, who was enjoying the roast pork.

"You can't change anything in life without a little work. I gave them a choice," said Thomas. "Either commit to a job or leave the country."

"And they abided by that?" pressed the president of India. His country had many unemployed souls.

"Not at first. Many rebelled, but some took positions they learned to appreciate. Our jails are empty, and very few crimes are committed." After locking eyes with every man at the table, Thomas picked up his fork and tried some of the smoked salmon.

The president of Haiti devoured some roasted potatoes before asking, "What do you do with the convicts?"

"If found guilty, they are escorted out of our country." Thomas cut his steamed broccoli into edible portions.

The president of Brazil interjected, "You're just sending your problems our way." To punctuate his statement, he allowed his knife to make a clunking sound as he dropped it onto his dinner plate.

"That's correct," said India's president. He held his fork and knife in the air to emphasize the point.

"Yes, I'm sorry." Thomas was concerned about this problem, but it was better they deal with the criminals than Baltia. "If you follow my decrees, your countries will be crime free too."

The Brazilian president thought for a moment. "Criminals would have no place to go."

"Yes, exactly," Thomas said, pointing his finger.

"Could we really stop crime?" asked the Haitian president.

"Why not?" answered Thomas. "You won't know until you try."

Everyone at the table considered Thomas's words as they silently and thoughtfully ate their meal. They didn't speak again until their plates were clean. A waiter, dressed in a uniformed black suit, arrived and removed their empty plates before glasses of bourbon were placed in front of the men.

As the men sipped the alcohol, they glanced about the room, searching for their wives. Once their glasses were empty, they strolled to the dancing area. Their wives glided over to them and encouraged them onto the dance floor.

The gala continued well into the early morning hours. Everyone enjoyed themselves immensely and sang the praises of Baltia's president. They fell into bed tired from dancing but optimistic about their future.

Chapter Three

Thomas and Leah were the last to leave the banquet. Both drunk, they basked in the glow and excitement of the night. They were escorted by his private guard into a waiting limousine and then home to the presidential residence. Although both were exhausted, Thomas brought up Leah's most hated subject.

It was an old and exasperating argument. Thomas dreamt of a house full of his offspring, but Leah denied this wish. Under no condition would she ruin her perfectly trim figure with a pregnancy. She kept herself fashionably thin, just shy of starving herself. Generally, she nibbled on pieces of cheese, almonds, and carrots throughout the day. The couple only ate their evening meal together.

Even though Thomas knew the response would be the same, he continually pushed the subject of children. Leah would ignore these attempts, hoping he would cease talking about it.

His fingers trembled as they trailed his wife's boney frame. All the alcohol he had drunk caused his hands to shake, but he could still feel his wife's soft skin.

Leah interrupted his pleasure and grabbed his hand, "You're drunk."

"So what? So are you."

"Did you buy more condoms?"

"No," said Thomas. He tried to massage her fingers until she pulled her hand away from him.

"Then you can forget about sex." Leah rolled away from him.

He stretched out his hand and rested it on her bottom. "Just once won't make a difference."

Knocking his hand off her body, she said, "I'm not taking a chance."

Not giving up, he pressed, "Let's take a chance. I would so love a son."

"I don't want children." Leah slid out of the bed.

"Wouldn't you love a daughter you could dress up?" As he slowly raised his torso into a sitting position, Thomas could feel the bed spin.

She hesitated and gazed at herself in the standing mirror. "Yes, it would be nice."

"So let's make love."

"I can't." She turned her body to the right then to the left in front of the mirror.

Thomas rolled out of their bed and stumbled across the floor to stand beside her. "Why not? Don't you think it would be wonderful to have children?"

The couple admired themselves in the large, oval mirror.

"Yes, but I'm not putting my body through that." Leah pressed her nightgown against herself and admired her thin frame.

Thomas flattened his hand on her stomach. "I'm sure you'll quickly regain your figure."

"But what if I can't? I'll be fat." She twisted and turned her nightgown.

"You'll never be fat." Thomas laughed and burped.

"But if I have a baby, I'll be fat."

Thomas rested his hands on her boney shoulders. "There's no guarantee."

"No, but I'm not taking a chance." Leah pushed him away.

Huffing and puffing, Thomas strode into his private bathroom and slammed the door shut before he turned on the shower. After disrobing, he allowed the hot water to cleanse his well-proportioned body. Angry with her response, he scrubbed his body with soap.

When he returned to the bedroom, Leah was asleep. He crawled in beside her. He gazed down at her attractive features and wondered why he remained married to her. He should have a wife who would bear him offspring. He so wished for a son he could mould to follow him in politics.

Because he was from a small family, Thomas hoped to bring forth a house full of children. He had become increasingly frustrated by Leah's consistent rejection of his advances; less and less he approached her with the suggestion of sex.

Sometimes Thomas wondered if Leah might be involved in an affair, but he tossed that thought out of his head. Leah had always maintained an aversion to sex. Even when they were first married, their unions were rare and infrequent. Leah would always put him off with the excuse of a headache, which only angered him and put him off the thought of having sex with her.

~

The next morning, after Thomas had left for the office, Leah slipped silently out of the rear of the house to make her way to the garage as inconspicuously as possible. She focussed on her surroundings, hoping no one saw her. It really didn't matter if she was spotted because she usually went out around this time, but she was about to commit a sin, and she preferred no one knowing.

She jumped into her pink Mercedes Sport that was parked between Thomas's ocean-blue Lexus and a black Jeep. Stopping to listen for a second, she slipped the key into the engine and turned it on with a click. The car purred as she manoeuvred it out of its parking space and into the quiet street. Consistent with her usual routine, she turned right onto a road leading into town.

As the house disappeared, Leah breathed deeply, as if she hadn't inhaled for a few minutes. Her mind played over the route she had taken so many times. No one seemed to notice her and she guessed she was safe, hoping no one would discover her secret.

After driving five blocks, she turned left and headed west. Periodically, she checked the car mirrors to make sure she wasn't being followed. Though she drove a very recognizable car, Leah wasn't overly concerned, but she made a number of quick turns just in case. No car was following; she was alone.

She often wondered what Thomas would do if he found out. He would, of course, divorce her immediately but she didn't let that dissuade her. Though she would never admit it out loud, Leah didn't love her husband anymore. However, she would never be the one to leave. She loved her high social position too much.

As she cleared a plot of trees, a severe stone mansion revealed itself. It stood in a patch of flat grassland further up the hill. Turning right into the paved driveway, Leah headed towards the back of the house where a small parking lot lay hidden.

Leah remained in her car for a few moments, listening for any sound. She couldn't hear anything but the musical chirping from the black and white sparrows in the trees. The impressive house was surrounded by a variety of ash and elm trees.

She jumped out of her car and walked into the mansion through the back door leading to the kitchen. After passing through another door, she made her way through a comfortable room with a moon-shaped leather couch. It faced a large sixty-inch television set. Beside the TV was an expensive stereo system. The only other thing in the room was a well-stocked liquor cabinet.

Upon reaching the main vestibule, she heard: "I'm in here."

The words came from the living room. The room was filled with creamy, white furniture giving the room a stark, severe tone. Few paintings adorned the walls, but they had a surreal quality due to their black and white compositions. It wasn't a style Leah would recommend but she wasn't here to comment on the home's contents.

Relaxing on the plush loveseat, the vice-president, Harmon Sinclair, stared at Leah with lust in his eyes. Harmon was of average height with thin black hair, which he kept short. Leah wouldn't call him handsome, but his looks were striking, maybe because of his intense stare. Their affair began two years ago. It was easy to maintain due to the president's busy work schedule and the many trips he took abroad. In the past, Leah had accompanied her husband on those trips, but now she complained about some ailment deterring her from travelling.

Lowering herself onto the loveseat, Leah leaned over and massaged Harmon's head with her manicured fingers. She plied his face with little smacking kisses, marking it with pink lipstick. He relaxed, hands on his lap, enjoying her playfulness.

After she gently massaged his shoulders, she trailed her finger down his body. Leah lowered her head and stared straight into his eyes. Harmon smiled, threw her back onto the luxurious couch, and almost strangled her while passionately kissing her neck. His lips moved further south and rested for a time on her lovely, small breasts.

Leah stopped his advances. Shaking her hips, she stood up and removed her grey silk dress. All that was left on her thin frame was black satin lingerie. She gently laid her clothes on the couch. Once she was sure her clothes wouldn't crease, she turned her attention to removing Harmon's strict, black suit. Once his clothes were off, they fell onto the floor, where their union was hot and passionate.

After both were satisfied, Harman grabbed a pack of cigarettes on the glass coffee table. Once had had lit one for Leah, he lit another for himself. The couple lay back, relaxing, and watching their smoke twist together and rise to the ceiling.

If Thomas ever saw Leah smoking a cigarette, he would be furious. He despised smoking and wouldn't allow it anywhere near him. He was pushing to have it abolished from his country, even though he understood the difficulties some people had with quitting the disgusting habit. Leah relished breaking her husband's rules, especially with the second most-powerful man in the country.

After putting out his cigarette, Harmon picked up the ashtray and held it for Leah to dispose of hers. He took her free hand and lifted it to his mouth, where he planted a sloppy kiss. He began to massage her buttocks, which fit perfectly in his large hands. He massaged slowly at first, and then he gathered speed as his passion grew. Without much preamble, Harmon thrust himself inside her. They rolled and rocked around on the carpeted floor until both screamed.

"Was that good for you?" Harmon murmured, brushing back his hair with his fingers.

"You know it was." A gratified smile played on her lips. "How long do we have?"

"No time at all. I have to get back to the office." He pulled his body forward and sat up. He used his arms to push off the floor and come to a standing position. He put out his hand to help Leah rise.

After Leah gathered her clothes and dressed, she sauntered over to the mirror to make sure everything was in order.

"You look delightful," admired Harmon. "Can you let yourself out?"

"Of course. I'll see you tomorrow." She slid out the back door and into her car.

Though the interaction was short, Leah was content. She loved her relationship with Harmon. He didn't waste time talking as her husband did. It drove her nuts having to listen to all the crap Thomas dealt with during the day. She just wasn't interested.

Harmon was perfect for her. She got what she wanted, and she didn't have to waste time. But she knew he was in love with her. He had yet to admit it, so Leah figured she was safe from having that conversation. She would never leave Thomas.

~

Watching her leave, Harmon thought about his feelings for her. He was in love with her, but he knew Leah did not love him, although she seemed to thoroughly enjoy their sexual adventures. It was true Harmon was a very powerful man; however, he came from meagre beginnings, which Leah found distasteful. Sex was fine, but Leah would never lower herself to marry a man with such a history.

Harmon Sinclair grew up as an only child in the poorest section of Graton, and he constantly complained about his limited environment. His parents ran a small vegetable stand in the local market. Every day, they encouraged people to buy their stock. They received their consignment from a local farmer who depended upon the Sinclairs to sell his produce.

Harmon hated the food stand and rebelled every time his parents expected him to help. Instead, Harmon spent much of his time reading anything he could find to propel him out of that horrible poverty. Since school was free to every child in the country, Harmon absorbed everything he was taught. Not a popular boy, he spent many hours alone at the school library. His ticket out was politics, and so began a long and arduous struggle.

Starting with Socrates, Aristotle, and Plato, Harmon read all their political writings. After he understood the classical philosophers, he turned his eyes towards Thomas Hobbes, Jean-Jacques Rousseau, and Immanuel Kant. He devoured their books, essays, and papers. A few years later, he began reading John Stuart Mill, Karl Marx, Friedrich Nietzsche, and Jean-Paul Sartre.

After absorbing these political geniuses, Harmon leaned towards dictatorship and studied Russian,

Italian, and German regimes. His goal was to recreate a form of government imposing strict and arbitrary rules for the people to follow. He would be in charge, a situation providing him the opportunity to live far beyond his meagre beginnings.

His affair with Leah also proved how far he had come. His ability to seduce the first lady gave him further reason to believe he could take over the position of president. He enjoyed his time with her, but he wished she would offer more, like stay the night, but she never did.

Harmon couldn't wait for Thomas to screw up. He disagreed with some of Thomas's policies, such as his ban on cigarettes, his decision to evict criminals, and having the government responsible for paying people's salaries.

Harmon's time would come.

Chapter Four

After a long, hectic day in the office, Harmon Sinclair's day was not as yet complete. He had one more meeting to attend, and it was a secret one. It wasn't written into any calendar and he hadn't told anyone about it.

It had been a difficult feat locating the right men to complete the task he required. Harmon spent many hours searching the internet and reached out to several sites, but no one replied to his emails. Then, perchance, he landed upon a simple site extolling the skills of two men. There were no pictures of any kind on the bland website.

Harmon was pleased when they responded to his email. Their profession was to rid the world of anyone they were paid to eliminate. Their resume was replete with people who no longer existed. Together, they were a dangerous team intent on completing every project assigned to them.

After a few short emails, they agreed to meet with Harmon in one week at a busy place where they could blend in. Evening would be the best time to meet because then their conference wouldn't look suspicious.

The week had passed and the meeting date was upon him. On a quiet stretch of road leading out of the city, Harmon entered a local tavern pleasantly situated in the middle of the highway. Le Lion was packed with locals celebrating the end of yet another day.

Though the bar was wide and open, it held little decoration on the stiff, brown walls. A few small chandeliers hung from the stark, black ceiling. A lone barman stood behind the long, high table top lined with drinks for his many customers.

After passing through the threshold, Harmon allowed his eyes adjust to the minimal light. He searched the patrons until he noticed two strange men in the corner booth. Guessing they were the men he was looking for, he walked towards them.

Both men had grisly scowls on their stern, closed faces, but that is where the similarities ended. One man was thin and ugly with deep scars on his face. He stood well over six feet tall with lanky arms and legs. Here was a man who would always look out of place. He was simply dressed in a rough, black woollen sweater and plain blue jeans, which had obviously seen many days.

The other man was better looking but had a few irregular twitches. He was constantly moving about in his chair, as if he sought the most comfortable position but never found it. Shorter than his partner by five inches, he was still an imposing figure. His well-built body was squeezed into a blue dress shirt that's buttons threatened to pop, and a new pair of blue jeans.

As Harmon approached the two dangerous men, it was obvious the pair had been waiting awhile because numerous beer bottles littered the table. Unconcerned, Harmon sat on the bench across from the assassins.

The men glared at each other from across the table. Harmon slid his arms along the messy surface, moving the empty bottles out of his way.

"Bob Gill," said the ugly man, nodding at Bob. "I'm Paul Thompson."

Harmon continued to stare at the men as if he already knew their names.

"We've been waiting for over an hour," said Bob, slamming his beer bottle on the table. "We were about to leave."

"You were paid to wait," said Harmon. He tried to appear calm and confident.

"Speaking of paid, when do we get our money?" asked Bob as he took another swig of beer.

"I'll give you half tonight and the other half when the deed is done."

Paul put out his hand. "Let's see that half."

Harmon reached into his breast pocket and pulled out a thick, white envelope. He placed it in the centre of the table.

Paul grabbed it, opened it, and flipped through the bills. He nodded to Bob.

Satisfied their fee had been paid, Bob raised his eyes to stare at Harmon. "What's the job?"

Harmon moved his hands onto his lap and rubbed them against his pants. He looked them straight in the eye. "I want you to kill Thomas Edmonds."

"The president?" Paul asked as he held his beer bottle in mid-air.

"Yes," Harmon replied. He placed another white envelope on the table. "Here's his itinerary for the next few days."

Paul opened the envelope and followed the lines of the president's duties. He showed the list to Bob, who scratched his two days' worth of stubble, and nodded.

Bob put his beer to his lips and drank deeply. After taking a breath, he said, "We'll want another two million."

"We agreed upon one million," Harmon protested. He straightened his back.

"Yeah, but you want us to the kill the president," Paul answered, fingering the envelope full of money.

"So what? It's all laid out for you." Harmon leaned back in the chair and crossed his arms against his chest.

"Not enough money," said Paul in a low, deep voice. He moved forward, narrowing the space between them.

Bob reached out his hand and touched Paul's shoulder as he stared at Harmon. "We'll never be able to return to this country after the deed is done. We require more money."

"Okay, another five hundred thousand."

"Two million," Bob repeated.

"One million," countered Harmon. He removed a pack of cigarettes from his suit pocket and lit one.

Bob and Paul glanced at each other.

"1.5 million," said Bob.

"One million." Harmon stood his ground and stared back at the men.

"Fuck it," said Bob. His eyes followed the smoke from Harmon's cigarette. "Okay, one million."

"Deal." Harmon held out his hand. Both men shook it, and the contract was sealed. "You'll get it with the final payment."

Paul's and Bob's smiles reminded Harmon of a grimace.

"I'll be here when you've completed the job," said Harmon. He rose and headed out of the bar.

As he reached the front doors, a small group of men entered and held the door open for him. After Harmon stepped over the threshold, he marched across the parking lot and jumped into his black Jaguar. He headed home feeling happier than he had in years. His devilish plan was going to work.

Chapter Five

A few days later, Thomas woke early. As he left his wife asleep in bed, he stretched and headed for the shower. With his eyes still closed and his head aching, he soaped his body and washed his hair. After rinsing, he finally opened his eyes and smiled. This was going to be a good day. He could feel it.

After devouring eggs over-easy, crispy bacon, and rye toast, he made his way to his office. Several government employees were already working at their desks. Numerous file cabinets and dark wooden tables lined the spacious room, allowing plenty of space to work.

The president unlocked his office and relaxed behind a massive oak desk covered with files and papers. He was dressed handsomely in an attractive, dark blue, three-piece suit with a white starched shirt and a colourful blue tie. As usual, a generous smile played on his face. His perfectly combed brown hair was in place and his face was clean-shaven.

He noticed a short line of people waiting to speak with him. His morning routine included making himself available to his citizens. Since most were content with their daily lives, only a few required his personal attention.

After an hour's discussion with a number of people, Thomas ruminated about one man's request. He had begged for permission to bring his wife's Syrian family to Baltia. They wished for a better life. The man worried about the dangerous situation there and wanted to please his wife by bringing her family to Baltia. Of course, Thomas conceded to the request. He felt bad for their troubles.

The last man entered his office and was shown to a black leather chair in front of Thomas's desk. The man waited for Thomas to acknowledge him.

"Your name and occupation, please?" Thomas asked, looking up from the papers in his hand.

"Michael Soros, sir. I'm the butcher."

"And how can I help you?" Thomas picked up a pen and a blank piece of paper.

"May we please speak in private?" Michael motioned to the assorted staff moving about the room.

Thomas glanced around and dismissed everyone with a sweep of his hand.

When the last person left and closed the door, Thomas asked, "Why the need for such privacy?"

"I have important and dangerous news for you," Michael said, looking a little nervous.

Waiting for Michael to calm down, Thomas said, "Please, go on."

Clearing his throat, Michael gathered himself together. "Two men are planning to kill you tonight when you go out for your evening run."

"What men?" Thomas dropped the papers in his hand and gave Michael his full attention.

"The assassins are Paul Thompson and Bob Gill. I can describe them for you."

"How did you come upon this information?" Thomas wrote down the men's names.

"I overheard them Friday night at the tavern." Michael still couldn't look the president in the eye.

"Would they remember you?" asked Thomas.

"No," said Michael. "They were very drunk and completely concerned with their own business. They must have thought the loud bar would drown out their voices."

Thomas moved out from behind his desk and came to stand before Michael. He reached out to shake Michael's hand. "Great job. I'm very grateful. What did they say?"

"They plan to overtake you when you enter the woods and stuff you into a car. After driving to the country, they will put a bullet in your head and leave you by the side of the road."

"Why do they want to kill me?" Thomas sat down beside him.

Looking at the floor, Michael murmured, "They were hired by someone very close to you."

Thomas's jaw dropped and his eyes grew wide. "Who hired them?"

"Someone you trust." Michael still couldn't look directly at the president.

Thomas placed his hands on the armrests of Michael's chair and stared at him. "Stop speaking in riddles, man. Who is it?"

Michael whispered, "Your vice-president."

"Harmon Sinclair?" Not waiting for his answer, Thomas stood up and paced about the room.

"Yes," Michael finally admitted.

Thomas stopped his wanderings to stand before a picture on the wall. The photograph showed him smiling widely beside the Austrian president and Harmon Sinclair, who looked stern.

"Thank you for this information. You'll be richly rewarded. If there is anything you need, please tell me."

"I'm in need of nothing," replied Michael.

Thomas understood Michael was a humble man. "Then I owe you a favour. Would you mind describing the assassins to my secretary?"

As Michael rose from his chair, the president placed a hand on his shoulder and gazed into his eyes. He saw only honest respect. This man could be trusted.

Guiding Michael out of his office, Thomas put him in touch with one of his staff who prepared composite drawings from Michael's descriptions. Thomas stood behind her and watched her hands work. He concentrated on Michael's voice, memorizing the assassins' appearances.

When the drawings were completed and Michael was about to leave, Harmon appeared in the main room. Immediately, Thomas moved to Harmon's side and guided him into his private office, away from Michael. He wasn't sure if Harmon noticed the man, but he hoped not.

After Harmon left the president's chambers, Thomas invited two of his personal guard into his office and divulged what he had learned from Michael. He ordered the guards to put together a special unit to stop the assassins.

Chapter Six

That night, after closing the office, Thomas kept to his regular routine. After changing into his grey sweatpants and sweatshirt, he made his way to the lake trail. He gazed around the area; he was completely alone.

During the day, the area was crammed with people out for a walk around the pristine lake where geese, ducks, and swans congregated. Many citizens walked their dogs or jogged, and women with baby strollers came to meet with other mothers.

However, at this time of night, the lake area was quiet and devoid of movement. Only a light breeze rustled the leaves on the trees. A full moon shone, lighting Thomas's way and giving him a clear view of the area.

As soon as he began running, his mind relaxed and he calmed down. He used this time to think about his day with simple clarity. Usually he focussed on the problems of his people, but tonight he mulled over the news about the assassins.

He had been surprised to learn of their deadly plot. He couldn't believe Harmon had hired the assassins; the man always seemed so eager to please and completed his work capably. He never heard a complaint from him, so why would Harmon want to kill him?

Despite his lack of concerns with Harmon, he didn't like the man. Harmon was too strict and unemotional. He never could figure out what the man was thinking. Also, he rarely smiled, which Thomas disliked.

But why would he want to kill me? The question rolled around in Thomas's brain. He thought back to every interaction with the man but couldn't detect any treacherous signs. He had assumed Harmon was happy with his situation.

Little did he know the truth.

Thomas had kept the news of the planned assassination to himself, and only his guards knew what was happening. He didn't want to give Harmon any opportunity to change his plans, and he didn't want him to have an inkling of what was about to happen.

His guards informed him they had a strategy to keep him safe. Although Thomas had no idea what was planned, he was told to just act natural and not to worry. They would take care of everything.

Once he reached the paved path, he used a wooden bench to stretch out his leg muscles. He did a few exercises to limber up, such as raising his knees high and stepping quickly on the spot for a few seconds. The air was fresh and cool, excellent for running. Because of his long stride, he made his way quickly around the lake.

The water rippled gently as small waves lapped the shore. Thomas enjoyed nature, especially at this hour when he was finally alone from the constant attention. The clean air invigorated him.

However, he remained somewhat nervous about tonight's exploit. He glanced about, searching for the assassins or his guards. Sometimes he turned and checked behind him to see if he was being followed. Even though he knew his men were out there, he felt alone.

Since he had no control over what was about to happen, he pondered what action he would have to take against Harmon. If the assassins revealed Harmon as their employer, he would have no choice but to arrest him. But if they didn't, perhaps it would give Thomas more time to figure out why Harmon wanted him dead.

Halfway around the lake, he entered a small, wooded area. From what Michael had said, this was the area where the assassins would be waiting, but he noticed nothing. The only sound came from ducks nesting beside the lake. He quickened his pace.

As soon as he passed a huge boulder, he felt something bite him in the neck. He immediately fell to the ground.

~

"I feel like celebrating," Harmon announced while pouring champagne into two flute glasses.

"What's the occasion?" asked Leah, who was spread out on his bed.

"All my dreams are coming true." He handed Leah a glass.

"Let's drink to that," Leah said as she touched her glass to his, making a clinking sound.

Harmon smiled and took a long sip. This was the best champagne money could buy, and he enjoyed the best. He reached for Leah's hand and played with her fingers.

"How would you like to marry me?" Harmon raised her hand to his lips and kissed it.

"I'm already married," she reminded him as she removed her hand from his grasp.

"Something could happen to him. Marry me?" Harmon wouldn't take no for an answer.

Leah stood up, leaving her glass on the bedside table. "What do you mean 'something could happen to him?'"

Harmon smiled. "You never know. He could die."

Leah furrowed her brow and narrowed her eyes. "Die? Thomas? You're crazy. He's in perfect health."

"Things happen."

"What have you done?" She reached for a cigarette.

She looked lovely standing there naked. He loved her body and often took pleasure in it, but it angered him she was married to Thomas. She had to marry him. She must be his. He hoped her continued presence implied she was considering his proposal.

"It's a secret, but you'll know soon enough." He grabbed the cigarette from her hand and watched her light another.

"Know what?" Leah took a long drag and stared at Harmon.

Ignoring her words, he said, "So? Will you marry me?"

"I'm not divorcing Thomas." Leah turned away and walked across the room.

"You don't love him. You love me," Harmon whined.

Leah turned around and gazed at him. "I don't love you either."

"That's pretty harsh." Harmon frowned.

Leah put her cigarette out in the glass ashtray. Straightening her back, she said, "He gives me everything I need."

"But what about our great sex?"

"What about it?" She shrugged her shoulders.

Taking a deep breath, he said, "You're cold."

"No colder than you." She smiled at him.

"We're a pair, aren't we?" He slid over to her, put his arm around her waist, and drew her to him.

After Leah quickly pecked him on the lips, she pulled away. "Enough for today. I have to go. But first I want to know what awaits me."

"You'll see." Harmon turned his back on her and plopped down on the bed.

"Tell me now."

"There are some things I won't tell you." He picked up a glass from the table and sniffed it to determine its contents. Realizing it was vodka, he brought the glass to his lips and drank.

Leah mumbled and grumbled as she left the room. He heard her slam the back door. *She'll return when she learns of Thomas's death.* He would be her rock, and she would become part of his life. He desperately wanted her to be his wife.

A thought made Harmon check his phone; the assassins might have left a message. He planned to meet them in the bar later to provide them with their final payment. He couldn't wait to hear about their success.

Chapter Seven

Thomas's first thought was *ouch*. As he slowly returned to consciousness, he realized he ached all over and his limbs felt tight and sore. He sensed the presence of someone by his side. Slowly, he opened his eyes and found himself blinded by a light. He raised his hands to cover his eyes. Someone barked a command and the light went out.

Tensing his muscles, he tried to sit up. A strong arm grasped his back and helped him to rise. When he bolted upright, he covered his face with his hands and groaned.

"What happened?" he said.

A guard dressed in military camouflage said, "You were tranquillized, sir."

Remembering, Thomas put a hand to his neck and tested the area for pain. Tentatively, he rubbed it. He gathered he was shot there. "Did you capture the assassins?"

"Yes, sir, we were successful."

Thomas drew his fingers through his hair and found an egg-sized bump on his scalp. After wincing, he asked, "How?"

"We surrounded the wooded area after locating the stolen vehicle and discovered the assassins hiding behind a large rock, ten feet from the running path."

"Were they aware of your presence?" Thomas slid across the table, allowing his legs to hang over the edge.

"No, sir, definitely not." The guard put a box under Thomas's feet to give him some support.

"Thanks. Then what happened?" Another guard handed Thomas a bottle of water. He took a deep gulp. He hadn't realized how thirsty he was.

"We watched as they brought out a tranquillizer gun and shot you."

"How did you know it wasn't a real gun?" Thomas felt a shiver go down his spine.

"We saw them load the darts." The guard took Thomas's empty water bottle and offered him a full one.

Thomas held up his hand at the water. "Haven't you got anything stronger?"

Prepared, a guard brought out a bottle of scotch and poured some into a glass, which Thomas finished off in one gulp. He motioned to the guard to pour more.

A guard spoke up, "While they were carrying you to their car, we ambushed them. They tried to pull out their guns, but they weren't fast enough."

"Excellent job, guys. Thanks." Thomas groaned. The drug was still in his system, and he felt terrible.

"Take it easy, sir," said the guard on his left.

Thomas tapped his shoulder. "Where are the assassins now?"

"Locked up in prison, sir," said the guard.

"Good. Can you take me to my office? I have a few calls to make." Thomas tried to jump off the table, but the guards restrained him.

They glanced at each other until one spoke up. "Sir, we think it's best if you go home."

Thomas breathed deeply. "Fine. Those calls can wait until tomorrow."

"Can you stand?" asked one of the guards, removing the box.

To prove his ability, Thomas slowly lowered his feet onto the ground. He tested his limbs and came to a standing position. "I guess I can."

The guards led Thomas to their car and drove him home. Since Thomas didn't feel very good, he didn't speak. The guards, understanding his feelings, kept silent. When they arrived at the presidential residence, Thomas shook their hands then gingerly walked inside.

The place was quiet and still. Most of the servants had gone home for the night, and his wife was nowhere to be seen. He paused in the dining room to pour himself a glass of bourbon. He was about to leave when he decided to take the bottle as well. He climbed the stairs to his bedroom.

Dropping his clothes onto a chair, he stepped into the shower. The water felt good. His right arm hurt when he lifted his hands to wash his hair. He would have to take it easy.

Once dry, he pulled on some black silk pajamas. After finishing the liquor in his glass, he poured himself another. He was standing in the middle of the bedroom when his wife appeared.

"What are you doing here?" Leah asked. She dropped the coffee cup she carried and it shattered on the ground, sending fragments everywhere.

"You weren't expecting me?" Thomas moved to stand before her.

"Yes, of course," she stammered. Her body noticeably shook.

He placed his hands on her shoulders. "What's going on?"

She slipped out of his grasp, grabbed a towel, and then dropped it on the floor. Coffee soaked the cloth, but the glass was everywhere. "Nothing, my dear. Just didn't hear you come in."

"I just got in." Thomas was suspicious. She knew something. "How was your day, dear?"

"Fine." She walked over to the intercom and instructed a servant to clean up the mess.

Thomas fell into a chair with his glass of bourbon and gulped down half the contents. "What did you do today?"

"Not much." Leah moved over to her makeup table and settled down upon the small, cushioned chair. While gazing at herself in the mirror, she said, "Had lunch with Alison. Then we went shopping."

"What did you buy?" He crossed his legs and folded his arms across his chest.

Brushing her hair, she said, "Just a few odds and ends."

"How much do these odds and ends cost?"

Leah frowned and rolled her eyes. She picked up her purse and withdrew a few receipts. "Here you go. It's all here."

"Thank you, my dear." He flipped through the papers and sighed loudly. He grabbed his briefcase, opened it, and then stuffed the receipts inside.

"How was your day?" Leah asked tentatively, peering at him through the mirror.

Watching her movements, he said, "Good. Just a normal day."

Leah opened a jar of cream and spread it on her face. "Nothing out of the ordinary happened?"

Thomas turned to look at her. "Nothing. Why?"

"No reason. Just wondered." Avoiding his stare, she slipped into bed and turned away from him.

Thomas strode to his side of the bed and sat down with a big sigh. He turned and swung his legs up onto the bed. He put out a hand and touched her back; her body tensed.

Resigning himself to sleep, Thomas couldn't get the thought out of his head that she was hiding something. He decided to speak to his guards in the morning and have her watched. Something was up, and he had to find out what was going on.

~

While the president and first lady slept, Harmon entered Le Lion. He gazed about the busy room. Since Bob and Paul hadn't arrived, he chose a table in the corner just vacated by a young couple. The assassins were due at any moment.

When the waitress approached, Harmon ordered a brandy. He was celebrating.

He watched the waitress weave her way around the customers to reach the bar. She said something to the bartender and he poured a liquid into a glass. She picked it up and made her way back to Harmon.

Slowly Harmon lifted the glass to his lips. He said a prayer hoping the assassination would be a success and then he gulped down the alcohol. Thomas was dead, and he would be made president. Soon, he would take over the country and create a dictatorship.

For a few moments, his mind drifted back through the years to all the planning required to reach this moment. He wasn't a popular man so there was no way the people would vote him into the presidency; he had to take it by force. He had almost succeeded with the last president, but the man was never alone.

After Thomas had won the election, Harmon figured he was capable of killing him. From the beginning of his presidency, Thomas spent many moments alone. After watching him for a few years, Harmon laughed at the amazing opportunities afforded to him.

The only problem was, over time, Harmon had grown to like the man. Thomas was easy to respect, and Harmon admired his hard work. Thomas had befriended the vice-president after he had proved his worth, so Harmon had decided to bide his time. Knowing the man better made it harder to kill him, but his desire to be president was stronger than his aversion to committing murder.

He drummed his fingers on the table. First, he tapped his index finger and then the middle one joined in the song. Finally, all five fingers took part in the melody. Harmon was excited. He couldn't sit still while waiting to hear of the assassins' success.

But, by the time he had ordered his third drink and the assassins still hadn't arrived, Harmon became nervous, thinking perhaps the mission had failed. But what could have gone wrong? Everything was in order, and Bob and Paul were experts. They had assured him the job would be completed.

As time passed and the pair didn't arrive, Harmon felt frantic. His skin became hot and clammy. His back hurt from sitting so straight in expectation. He was stuck to his seat and couldn't get up. He decided to wait a little longer. He didn't want to leave for fear of missing them. He was sure they would arrive at any moment.

The bar slowly emptied. Only one table remained occupied by three drunken men. Everyone else had left for their warm beds. Harmon stared at the drunks. They didn't appear to be in any hurry to leave. One stuck up his arm and ordered more drinks.

The bartender walked over to the men. "You guys have had enough. Go home."

Laughing, the men stood up, knocking over their chairs. They stumbled out of the bar, arguing loudly about the best way to get home.

Harmon was alone. He glanced about the place, and his nose crinkled at the smell of stale cigarette smoke and spilt beer. He watched the bartender pick up the fallen chairs and lay them on the table. He retrieved his broom and began to sweep.

Something was wrong. Where were the assassins? What had happened to them? He picked up his glass, but the alcohol was long gone. He realized he had finished off five glasses. He couldn't think straight and his body felt wobbly, but he had to wait for the assassins. They would come. They would want the rest of their money. He was sure they would appear.

Harmon couldn't move; he felt frozen. He rubbed his face with his hands, trying to bring back some feeling. He was terrified the assassins had been discovered. What would happen if the president knew he had planned the assassination?

What should he do? How could he face Thomas? The questions raced around in his drunken mind. He would be put to death as a traitor if he were found out. He didn't want to die.

Out of the silence, the bartender said, "Isn't it about time you left?"

Harmon jumped at the sound of the man's voice. He tried to speak, but no words came out. After he cleared his throat, Harmon tried again. "Yes," he squeaked. "I'll go."

Placing his hands on the table, he straightened his legs. The bartender put out a hand to stop him from falling over. Gathering himself together, Harmon walked towards the door. With each step, it became easier to move, and he left the bar.

The cold night air hit him hard, like a slap in the face, which seemed to revive him somewhat. When he reached his car, he rolled down the windows and rested there, breathing deeply. His body shook, but Harmon didn't know if it were from fear or the cold.

He put his seat belt across his body, turned on the motor, and drove home, not knowing what to expect. Would the police be there waiting for him? Would he be put in jail and then hanged?

As he pulled into his driveway, the house was dark. No police waited for him by the front door or in the back parking lot. He strode into his house, fearful of what he would find.

Chapter Eight

The next morning, Thomas rose quietly and left his sleeping wife in bed. After he showered and dressed, he ate a quick breakfast of eggs and toast, then made his way to his office. He wondered what he would say to Harmon when they met at the ten o'clock cabinet meeting. The chance of talking privately was slim, but he wondered how Harmon would behave.

Sitting behind his desk, he concentrated on the new private bill being put forward by the doctors. They appealed to the government to inoculate every citizen with a new vaccine eradicating influenza. It was used in other countries, and the doctors wished for permission to give it every citizen for free. Thomas was sure the bill would easily pass.

Soon, the government employees arrived, and everyone took their positions in the main office. As was routine, Thomas greeted them and gave them their daily instructions. He had three meetings to attend: one with his cabinet ministers, one with the delegation from Russia, and the last with a group of Japanese businessmen. He made sure all the necessary papers were organized for each meeting.

At a quarter to ten, Thomas gathered all his needed files and put them in his briefcase. He took the elevator down to the ground floor where the council hall was located. Most of the cabinet ministers were already in their places. Thomas noticed Harmon's seat was vacant and wondered if he would have the nerve to show up.

Just before the clock struck ten, Harmon entered the hall and quickly made his way to his seat. He did not glance at Thomas, and Thomas only peeked at him through his peripheral vision. He wished to see if Harmon would give himself away.

The first matter on the agenda was the building of a new highway between the two southern cities. The highway was crumbling and was just not large enough for the many vehicles going back and forth. Both mayors had agreed to it, and the cabinet concurred.

Next, the cabinet discussed trade with Japan. The Japanese were interested in buying their cloth, which was the finest in the world. Thomas was meeting with them later in the day, along with the minister of foreign affairs, who spoke in great detail about the new opportunity to reach Asia.

Thomas glanced over at Harmon, but he never raised his hand to speak or made any comments to those sitting near him. Usually, he was very involved with each motion and spoke his mind, but today, he just stared down at the papers on his desk. Thomas enjoyed his discomfort. He hoped to see him struggle.

The last matter on the agenda was a discussion about their immigration requirements. The minister of immigration stood up and announced their new citizens were all gainfully employed and improving their lives in Baltia. For a while, the cabinet ministers discussed the best formats for immigration.

Just before the cabinet was dismissed, six of Thomas's personal guards entered the chamber. The head guard approached Thomas. He leaned forward to speak in Thomas's ear, and the two spoke for a minute. No one could determine what was being said. After Thomas nodded, the guard approached the cabinet. He wore his ceremonial uniform, and his black jacket was covered in colourful ribbons and cords. He cut a brilliant figure.

"There has been an assassination attempt made against our president." He spoke clearly and with composure.

Everyone stood at their desks, raised their arms and screamed in shock and anger.

Turning to stare at Thomas, one minister spoke up, "How are you, Mr. President? Obviously, it was unsuccessful, but what happened?"

"I was shot with a tranquillizer gun and abducted," replied Thomas.

A roar of displeasure shot around the room.

Thomas enjoyed the ministers' clamour. He revealed the story as told to him by his guards. "They saved my life."

The hall erupted with applause.

Thomas thanked everyone for their concern and assured them he was fine. "After a good night's sleep, I awoke recovered."

"Where are the assassins now?" asked the minister of natural resources.

The guard bowed and said, "We have them locked up and in seclusion at the prison."

"Are you a hundred percent sure these men are the culprits?" asked the justice minister.

"Yes," the guard confirmed. "They were caught in the act."

The minister of defence jumped up and bellowed, "They must be interrogated and then put to death."

"Our punishment for treason is death by hanging," said the justice minister. "Do we all agree?"

Every minister yelled their assent.

"Did they act on their own accord? Or were they hired by someone?" enquired the minister of health.

The guard cleared his throat and said, "We're not sure. The assassins aren't talking."

Thomas stared at Harmon. His face showed no emotion, but he was rapidly tapping his pen on his desk. Thomas hoped the man was scared. He must suffer for what he had done.

"You must interrogate them to find out the truth," insisted the minister of public services.

The minister of immigration raised his hand. "You must apply all pressure to learn who hired them."

"Yes," agreed the minister of defence. "Even if that means torture."

"Torture?" the minister of education asked. "That practice hasn't been used in centuries."

"We must discover the truth," insisted the minister of justice.

Thomas glanced at Harmon, who was sitting very still. Thomas wondered what he was thinking.

"I think we all agree," said the justice minister.

Every hand was raised into the air.

"Then it's settled," concluded the minister of justice. "Guard, do whatever is necessary to find out who hired the assassins."

The guards grabbed their rifles and raised them to their chest. They bowed, turned, and left the cabinet chamber.

The room erupted into noise as everyone talked at once. Thomas sat back in his chair and watched the proceedings. No president had ever been assassinated in Baltia, and the ministers yelled it wouldn't happen now.

"The vice-president has been silent today," the minister of foreign affairs pointed out.

Everyone looked at Harmon, whose face fell at being mentioned. Though his eyes bulged, the rest of his face showed no emotion. Thomas held his breath, waiting to hear what he would say.

Adjusting his tie, Harmon said, "Nasty business. I'm in total agreement. There's nothing for me to add. You seem to have things well in-hand."

Conversations broke out around the room. Thomas stood up and held out his hands. Everyone went silent.

"Let's wrap this up," said Thomas. He wasn't ready to put Harmon on the spot, and he intended to wait until the assassins had been interrogated. "There's nothing further to discuss. We'll let you know what the guards discover."

Eventually, the cabinet ministers left the hall and returned to their offices. Thomas watched Harmon jump out of his chair and join the mass moving out of the chamber.

Throughout the day, Thomas anxiously awaited to hear from the guards. The day passed by quickly and, before he knew it, he was alone in his office. After pouring himself a glass of rye, he took off his shoes, lay back in his chair, and rested his stocking feet on the messy desk. He hoped the guards would be able to extract the truth from the assassins.

Just as he was about to lock up his office, two of his guards presented themselves at his door. They waited for him to acknowledge them.

Thomas nodded and said, "What did they say?"

"We got nothing," said one of the guards.

"Nothing?"

The men bowed their heads, obviously dejected they had failed.

"May I speak with them?" Thomas wondered if a direct confrontation might reveal something.

"If you wish, sir," said a guard.

Thomas put on his coat and shoes, followed the guards to their car, and drove to the country's only prison.

Even though crime had been eliminated, one prison was kept open. It was very modern with the highest security, built on top of a hill on the eastern border. The cells were clean and freshly painted, and the bars were made from the strongest existing material.

The guards escorted Thomas into the prison's basement, where the assassins were being held. They opened a door leading to an interview room, where a metal table stood with two metal chairs, one on either side. The room was stark, bare, and smelled of bleach.

"We'll bring the criminals in one at a time," said a guard.

Thomas watched as an ugly man with chains on his arms and legs was dragged into the room and pushed onto the chair. A guard stood on either side of him with one hand on each shoulder to keep him from moving.

Placing his hands on the table, Thomas gazed straight into the man's face and said, "Do you know who I am?"

Staring back, the ugly man replied, "Yes."

"Why did you try to kill me?"

"We were hired to kill you."

"By whom?"

The man slowly raised his head and stared blankly into Thomas's eyes. He said nothing.

"Speak!" demanded Thomas.

"I'll take that secret to my grave," spat the ugly man.

"Then death it will be. Take him away," he instructed the guards.

The guards removed him and put him back into his cell. The other assassin was brought into the room, but he also said nothing. Thomas wondered why these horrible men would be so loyal to Harmon. What leverage did Harmon have over them?

His thoughts weighed heavily on him. He didn't know how he could accuse Harmon without implicating Michael. If Harmon had no qualms about killing him, then Michael's life would be in danger if his involvement was revealed. Thomas had no idea what he should do next.

Chapter Nine

Thomas didn't sleep well. He tossed and turned all night, so he was tired when he got up in the morning. His day wasn't any easier since there was so much to accomplish. He was glad when his day was completed and he could return home.

Heading straight for his study, Thomas fell exhausted into his dark brown chair. This was the one place he could call his own. Bookcases with first edition novels covered one wall. A large, antique wooden desk he had bought from an estate sale was set against the far wall. In the fireplace, a roaring fire burned.

He took off his suit jacket and laid it on the other chair. After twisting his head back and forth, he undid his tie to allow his neck to move easier. He stretched out his legs and sighed.

A few moments later, his butler arrived with a glass of whiskey on ice. He laid the drink on a small table beside Thomas and waited for any further instructions.

"Is my wife home?" Thomas asked as he brought the glass to his lips. He gulped down half the liquid before setting it back onto the table.

"Yes, sir," replied Arthur.

"Will you please ask her to join me?"

"Right away, sir."

"And bring me another glass. No, bring the bottle."

Arthur turned on his heels and made his way out of Thomas's study. He bumped into the housekeeper in the hall and asked her for Leah's location.

"She's in her bedroom, trying on some new dresses," replied the housekeeper.

Arthur made his way up the stairs to the second floor and knocked on the door to the main bedroom. He waited a few minutes until a maid opened the door.

After taking a few steps into the bedroom, he noticed Leah standing before her large oval mirror, admiring a new dress.

"Excuse me, ma'am," Arthur began.

Leah twirled, allowing the dress to float into the air. "What is it, Arthur?"

"Your husband requests your presence in his study."

Looking at Arthur's reflection in the mirror, she said, "Tell him I'm busy."

"Yes, ma'am."

Arthur turned briskly and strode out of the bedroom. He bounded down the stairs, and before returning to Thomas's study, he grabbed the bottle of whiskey. He knocked twice on the study door and let himself in.

"Well?" asked Thomas, rubbing his cold hands near the warm fire.

Arthur cleared his throat. "She's busy."

Thomas perched himself on the edge of his chair and slapped his hands on his thighs. "What do you mean 'busy?' I want her here now."

"She's trying on some dresses, sir."

How dare his wife refuse his request? He rarely asked anything of her. He thought she would be pleased he wanted to see her; her behaviour angered him.

"I don't care what she's wearing," barked Thomas. "Tell her to come here immediately."

Arthur left the liquor bottle on the table and headed out of the study. Closing the door behind him, he walked towards the stairwell and bumped into the housekeeper again.

"What's up?" Margaret asked, noticing Arthur's speed.

"There's a storm brewing," murmured Arthur with one foot on the staircase.

"What's she done now?"

"She refused a command. I better get going." Arthur raced up the stairs, leaving Margaret standing there.

When he reached the bedroom door, he knocked twice, and the maid opened the door. Leah still stood admiring herself in the mirror. Another maid was by her side, diligently testing the dress to make sure it fit properly.

Arthur took a few steps into the room and cleared his throat.

"What is it, Arthur?" Leah asked, twisting and turning showing off a splendid, light blue gown.

"Your husband requests your presence in his study."

Leah laughed, though it sounded more like a snarl. She pushed the maid away from her and turned towards Arthur with her hands on her hips. "Tell him I'm busy."

"Excuse me, ma'am, but I already told him. He insists you come down immediately. You can wear anything you want."

Leah spun around to look into the mirror again. She gazed at her reflection. Keeping her body straight, she only turned her head to stare at Arthur. "I don't think so. Tell him I'll be there when I'm ready."

"Yes, ma'am." Arthur left the room. He took the steps two at a time. When he reached Thomas's study, he tugged at his suit, adjusted his tie, and then knocked twice on the door. Hearing no sound, he opened the door and walked briskly across the threshold.

Arthur noticed Thomas was still sitting in his chair by the fire, pouring himself another glass of whiskey. Thomas didn't turn his head when he said, "Well?"

"She'll be down when she's ready," said Arthur, repeating her exact words. He stood erect, barely moving a muscle.

Jumping up, Thomas dropped his glass, which shattered into pieces. Arthur sprang to clean it up.

Ignoring Arthur, Thomas paced about the study, thinking about his wife's disobedience. He was furious.

Arthur placed the broken glass into the garbage and used a towel to clean up the liquid.

"Go one more time and demand she attend me." Thomas ordered.

Arthur nodded his head and, for the third time, left the study to climb the steps to the second floor. This time he climbed a little slower. As a man in his sixties, he found this undertaking a little tiring.

Again, he knocked twice on the bedroom door and, again, the maid opened it for him. Leah wore a yellow dress this time and still stood before her mirror.

"Why are you back?" Leah asked, obviously vexed.

"For the last time, the president has demanded your attendance," said Arthur.

Leah's throat made a low, deep chuckle that sounded sinister. She laid her hands on her hips and pushed her fingers towards each other against her flat stomach. Without taking her eyes off her reflection in the mirror, she said, "I'm busy."

Arthur couldn't believe what he was hearing. He stood there with his arms hanging at his sides. He was terrified to return to Thomas with only those words.

"What are you waiting for?" Leah asked.

"That's it? That's all I tell him?" implored Arthur. He shook in his shoes.

"That's it."

"I can't go back to him with only 'I'm busy.'" Arthur brought his hands together as if in prayer.

Leah ignored him as she searched through the other dresses hanging on a metal clothes rack. After she picked out a grey dress, she held it against her body.

"Do you like this colour on me?" she asked the maid.

"No, ma'am."

"Why not?" Leah continued to hold the dress before her and admire herself.

"I like this one better for you," said the maid as she picked out a dark blue dress and held it out to her.

"I still want to try on this grey one." Leah was about to go behind the screen to change dresses when she noticed Arthur still standing there.

"What are you doing? Can't you see I'm busy?"

"Yes, ma'am; I know, ma'am. But I need to tell him something other than you're busy," pleaded Arthur.

"Tell him," she hesitated. "Tell him I'll see him at dinner."

Arthur hunched his shoulders, clasped his hands behind his back, and walked out of the bedroom. He returned to the stairwell and slowly stepped down one step at a time.

When he reached the ground floor, he found Margaret standing there with a small tray and a glass.

"I thought you could use this," said Margaret, holding up the tray.

Arthur picked up the glass, smelt it, and then smiled at Margaret. "You're a treasure." He drank down the scotch, giving him the fortitude he needed to face Thomas.

"What's going on?" Margaret asked.

"The first lady has ignored her husband's command to attend him three times now."

"What's the matter with her?" Margaret accepted the empty glass from Arthur. She held onto the glass, but she tucked the tray under her arm.

"I don't know. She seems to take joy in vexing him. He doesn't ask much of her." Arthur smacked his lips.

"She's too arrogant to realize how good she has it." Margaret shook her head to show how much she didn't understand her.

"That's true," he agreed. He took a deep breath. "I have to face the president."

"Do your duty. You can do no more."

"I know." He smiled a little mournfully. Patting Margaret on the arm, he headed off to Thomas's study.

He knocked twice. After waiting a few minutes, he opened the door and let himself in. Thomas was now sitting behind his desk, working on his laptop. He seemed quite absorbed and didn't acknowledge Arthur's presence.

Arthur noticed the whiskey bottle was almost empty. Not knowing what to do, he took two steps forward to stand directly in front of the massive, paper-strewn desk.

"I know you're there," Thomas barked. He glanced over the computer screen. "Where is she?"

"She said she'll see you at dinner."

"And that's the only reply I receive?" Thomas leaned back in his chair but moving made his head spin. He bolted upright and tried to straighten his back.

Arthur nodded. "Anything further I can do for you, sir?"

"No, thank you, Arthur. That will be quite enough. I know you're exhausted. Go relax. I won't need you any further tonight."

Arthur had a little trouble understanding Thomas because he slurred his words, but he was relieved he was free from the conflict.

"Goodnight, sir." Arthur left the study, headed to his quarters, and did as he was told. After he had taken off his shoes and jacket, he lay down on his bed, briefly wondering what would happen next. He soon fell asleep.

Chapter Ten

After an exhausting day of trying on a variety of dresses, Leah picked the dark red one to wear to dinner. She had her maid find the perfect black shoes from her closet. Another maid expertly applied her makeup and styled her hair. Once she felt her appearance was perfect, she left her bedroom, glided down the stairs, and into the dining room.

Thomas was already settled in his seat at the head of the table. He slowly rose from his chair to acknowledge her. She nodded in response and took her place at the other end of the long, wooden table.

Gracefully, she lowered herself into the high-back, wooden chair and lightly placed her napkin upon her lap. She gently rested her bare arms on the white tablecloth and waited for the waiters to serve them their dinner. Thomas's shoulders were slouched, and his head bobbed a bit. He seemed preoccupied with something and didn't speak.

Two waiters appeared, each carrying a plate of food. One lay a plate before Thomas, and the other placed one in front of Leah. The men silently moved out of the dining room and returned to the kitchen.

Leah's dinner plate included lettuce, tomatoes, cucumber, red peppers, and a couple of kinds of cheese. She picked up her fork and speared a piece of Swiss cheese. She nibbled on it until it had shrunk in half. Then she took the rest into her mouth.

Thomas's plate was more substantial. He had received a steak, medium rare, as well as steamed green beans and scalloped potatoes. He devoured the meal.

All during the dinner, the room stayed quiet. The only sound heard was the clinking of their cutlery against their plates.

Once Thomas had cleaned his plate and Leah had eaten half her salad, the waiters appeared and removed their plates. Leah tapped her mouth with her napkin and laid it on the table. Thomas wiped his hands, folded his napkin, and placed it in front of him.

He rubbed the stubble on his unshaven face and pushed out the words: "Busy day?"

She gazed into his reddened eyes and smiled sweetly. "Yes, dear, very busy."

"And what were you so busy doing?" Thomas smiled back as charmingly as he could.

"We have all those weddings coming up and the mayor's dinner next week. I needed some new dresses. You know I have to look my best." She plucked at her dress as if to remove non-existent fluff.

"Do you really need a new dress for every affair?" He tried to add up the sums in his head, but his brain was too sluggish.

"Of course I do, dear." She laughed, but no sound came out.

Thomas shook his head. "What do you do with them?"

Her blue eyes turned upwards, and she smiled. "They're in my closet."

"Your closet must be full." He put his hand to his mouth to hold in a small burp.

"Actually, dear, it is. That's something I'd like to discuss with you." With her elbows on the table, she tried to seduce him with her eyes.

He leaned back with an air of interested expectation. "And what would that be?"

"I was thinking of turning the parlour off the bedroom into a closet." She smiled again, as if to imply she would get her way.

Thomas huffed. "You need something that big?"

"I do." She placed her hands under her face.

"Enough." Thomas pulled himself erect.

"What do you mean, dear?" She asked while tracing her lovely face with a slender finger.

"No more." He pounded the table with his fists. "I've had enough."

Startled by his anger, she asked, "Enough with what, dear?"

Thomas stuck his hands on the table, moved his head forward, and stared straight at her. "I've had enough of you."

She laughed. "Oh, sweetheart, how can you say that?"

He stood up, wobbled, and reached for the back of the chair. "I'm filing for divorce."

Her face turned a bright shade of red, and her voice squeaked, "Oh no, dear. How can you do that?"

"Very easily," he said, turning his back on her.

Jumping out of her chair, she ran to him. She reached out and put a hand on his arm. "You love me, don't you?"

He shook her hand off his arm. "No, not in years."

She let a tear seep from her eye. "Where am I to go?"

"I don't care." He took a step forward. "Move back in with your parents."

Her mouth dropped. "But they live in New York."

"The farther you are from me, the better." He walked away, putting some distance between them.

Leah shouted at his back, "How can you say this? You don't really want to divorce me."

Thomas turned around and said, "Watch me."

"*Thomas!*" she screamed.

Thomas shook his head. "It's over. Start packing."

He strode out of the dining room, leaving Leah with her mouth wide open. She hung her head and cried.

When the kitchen staff entered the dining room to clear the table, she ran to her bedroom. She grabbed her suitcases from the top shelf of her closet and packed everything she would need for a few days. Her maids could finish the rest and send everything to wherever she ended up.

She wasn't worried. He would come around. Of course he loved her; he wouldn't divorce her. He was drunk, and that's why he was so angry. Once he sobered up, he'd contact her and apologize. She was sure.

~

When Thomas awoke the next morning, his clear head reminded him of the night before. He had reacted a little harsher than normal, but his resolve was definite.

He contacted his lawyers to begin divorce proceedings. He and Leah had agreed to a prenuptial agreement where both parties retained what they brought into the marriage and Leah would be paid a decided amount in alimony until she married again.

The divorce proceeded quickly and efficiently. Leah's lawyer had no choice but to agree to all Thomas's concessions. Thomas thought this was a little suspicious, but he had no interest in finding out what else she had done.

He hid in his study while Leah moved her belongings out of the presidential house. He didn't care what she took and allowed her free reign. She left a short note in the hall stating she had moved into a friend's condominium. She would remain there until she decided where to go.

Her recent behaviour only enforced Thomas's belief he could do without her. He required a woman who would bear him children and stand by his side. Once the divorce went through, Thomas heaved a huge sigh of relief and optimistically looked towards his future with a new wife.

Chapter Eleven

"Why don't you date?" asked Martin, Thomas's younger brother.

The men were relaxing over a brandy at the end of another busy day. The brothers had formed a habit of spending more time together since Leah's departure. At the end of each day, Thomas enjoyed talking over his schedule with his younger brother and obtaining his advice.

"It's not easy for me to date," replied Thomas. He twirled his glass in the air, allowing the fire's glow to shine through it.

"Of course you can. There are plenty of single, available women in this country."

"I know, but will they love me for me, or because I'm the president?" Thomas put the glass to his lips and sipped.

"Yes, definitely a problem, but you have to try." Martin held up his glass and took a big gulp.

"I know." The thought rolled around in Thomas's head. Because of Leah, he felt nervous trusting another woman. He had to remind himself Leah was the worst offender and all women weren't like her.

"Cheer up, Thomas. Leah wasn't right for you, and you know that," Martin interjected, reading his brother's thoughts.

Thomas shook his head. "I should never have married her."

He thought back to the first time he saw Leah. It was at a ball in New York City given for the US ambassador. She had accompanied her father and was dressed in a shockingly sheer, tight, white gown. He noticed how women flocked around her. He was introduced by his ambassador who had dealings with her father.

Thomas had been impressed with her firm handshake and the way she gazed straight into his eyes, almost daring him not to fall in love with her. He succumbed to her brilliant appearance and fell in love immediately. She was nothing like any woman he had ever met. He pursued her relentlessly until she gave in and agreed to be his wife.

He had been blinded by her outward appearance and, therefore, he missed her many faults. He had to find a woman he could love unconditionally and trust completely. He needed someone who would share in his life as his lover, partner, and best friend. And she must bear him children. He mourned the lost past when he could have started a family.

"No regrets. She served her purpose, and now it's time for you to meet your soulmate." Martin rose from the chair, walked over to the bar, and grabbed the bottle of brandy. He poured himself a full glass, walked over to Thomas, and held up the bottle.

Thomas lifted his glass. He watched his brother refill it. "You really believe that?"

"Yes, I do. When I met Janet, I knew I had found my soulmate."

Martin had introduced his girlfriend, Janet, to Thomas after their second date. They had met while in university and immediately became a couple. Janet was an intellectual who treated people equally, which had impressed Thomas. She came from a good family of comfortable means, and she didn't go crazy with Martin's wealth as Leah had with his. The two women had never been friends.

Mulling over all of this, Thomas said, "She's good for you. I'd love to find someone like her."

"She's the perfect wife, and I love her more each day. I want you to find that kind of love." Martin shook his glass to warm up his brandy.

Thomas coughed. "But I just can't ask any woman out."

Taking a sip to wet his dry throat, Thomas realized his tight shoulders felt sore from the stress. He was anxious to find the right woman to be his partner. It was an important position, and he had to be careful whom he chose.

"Why not?" Martin scrunched his nose and closed his eyes.

Shaking his head, he said, "I'd feel awkward."

Martin put his hand to his head and thought for a moment. "You need the proper setting to meet your perfect woman."

"What kind of setting?" He liked where this was heading. His brother could always be counted on to come up with great ideas.

Martin stood up and took a step towards the roaring fire. "Why not host a beauty pageant and invite every single woman in the country?"

Thomas laughed. "Isn't that a bit obvious?"

Martin turned back towards his brother. "Sure, but think of it."

Thomas rubbed his chin. "That does sound good."

"Of course it does." Martin gave his brother a big smile. "And you are a little shallow."

Thomas laughed. He couldn't hide anything from his brother. "Yes, I want an attractive woman, but she must have a mind."

"Then hold a beauty pageant."

"Not a bad idea at all," said Thomas. He jumped up from his chair and moved over to his desk. He opened his laptop and made some notes.

The next day, he called his personal staff into his office. They took their seats around his desk, waiting expectantly.

Thomas gave them a sublime smile. "Welcome, everyone. I have decided we should hold a beauty pageant with a victory ball afterwards. Every single woman in the country may compete. But I want it understood: intelligence is just as important as beauty. Please set it up."

The staff glanced at each other.

"I think that would be a fine idea," said one of the secretaries while she made notes on a pad of paper.

"It shall be done," affirmed another.

His staff quickly rose from their chairs and left Thomas's office. They were eager to host the best event ever, since it was clear the winner would be the new first lady.

They needed judges for the contest. The staff put their heads together and chose the head of police, Brett Holsen; the bronze medallist at the World Cup of skating, Anna Kesti, who was the country's sweetheart; and the youngest general in Baltia's military, General Arthur Blackwood. One staff member contacted them and confirmed they would accept the position of judge for the beauty pageant.

Two staff members composed the official announcement. One person arranged for the city's grand hall to be used for the event, and organized the stage, as well as the seating arrangements. Box seats were saved for the president, Martin, and his wife.

When all was decided, they picked a date in August for the pageant. The staff believed they would have enough time to prepare for the event. One secretary wrote a memo to the president detailing their efforts. They hoped he would be pleased, and he was.

Once the word was out, it spread throughout the country. Everyone was thrilled with the news because any reason for a party was a good one. People counted down the days until the pageant since they understood the importance of the event.

Chapter Twelve

When Michael Soros heard about the beauty pageant, he knew exactly what to do with the news. His cousin, Katie, had been living with him since she was a child, and now, at the age of twenty-three, she would be perfect for the contest.

Like the rest of the populace, he understood the winner would become the new first lady. Because he had saved the president's life, he hoped the president would repay him and pick his cousin as his wife.

Katie had lost her parents in a horrific car crash, and, at the tender age of ten, she had found herself alone. She contacted Michael, who lived in Graton, with the hope she could move in with him because he was alone, too. His wife had died a few years before, and his children lived in their own homes. Katie wished for a better life in the city. There was nothing left for her in the country.

Michael had looked forward to Katie's company. Anna, his beautiful wife, had died from cancer and he missed a female in the house. His elder daughter, Portia, was married and had just birthed her first child. His younger daughter, Martha, was finishing her law degree and lived with her boyfriend, an environmental lawyer.

On the date of Katie's arrival, he had met her at the train station. It had been a few years since his cousin had brought his family to visit them in the city, but Michael recognized Katie immediately when she stepped off the train. She looked so much like her mother. She wore a simple blue dress and a smart pair of sandals. Her long brown hair hung down her back and her brown eyes were warm.

He picked up her suitcase, put it in the trunk, and then opened the passenger door for her. As soon as he closed her door, he moved over to the driver's side, jumped in, and then put on his seat belt. He smiled over at Katie and asked, "Ready?"

"I'm so ready." She laughed.

Michael smiled. "Moving to the big city will be quite a change for you."

"Yes, I know, but I'm prepared for whatever will happen." Her head kept turning so she could stare out the front and side windows.

"That's the King August Hotel," he said when he noticed her eyes widen and her mouth drop.

"Magnificent," was her only reply.

"I hope you'll be happy with me. I live a simple life."

"Thank you, I will." Katie paused. "And thank you for all your help with the funeral."

"I was glad to help." He glanced at her sideways, hoping the topic wouldn't be too difficult for her.

She wiped a tear from her eye.

Michael glanced in his rear-view mirror, and then over to Katie. "Hopefully this new life is just what you need." Michael turned his eyes back on the road since traffic was heavy.

"Yes, I'm sure. I'm very hopeful."

That was thirteen years ago, but Michael felt like it was just yesterday Katie had come to live with him. They enjoyed their life together and became close friends. Katie was a sweet girl who only improved Michael's simple existence.

Because she had such a special connection with children, she decided teaching would be the perfect occupation. So, at twenty, she completed university, and then found a job teaching grade three. Katie loved her class and her wonderful life.

Holding onto the flyer with the announcement of the beauty pageant, Michael approached Katie when she returned from school.

"Welcome home, my dear," he said as she walked in the door.

"Thank you, cousin. I'm glad to be home. Do you need anything?"

He pulled out the flyer and handed it to her. She accepted the pretty paper and read its contents. Upon finishing, she frowned.

"I can't attend a beauty contest," she said, handing the advertisement back to Michael.

"Why not?" Michael was surprised at her response.

Katie lowered her eyes. "I have nothing to wear."

"Then we'll get you new clothes."

"I can't ask that of you."

"Of course you can. I'd love to see you happily married. Maybe even to the president."

"He would never be interested in me." Katie blushed and put up her hands to cover her red cheeks.

"You never know." Michael smiled like he had a secret.

"Don't be silly. I'm not classy enough to marry the president. His ex-wife was the most elegant woman in the country. She also came from the upper-class. I'm no one."

"Don't put yourself down, Katie. You have many wonderful attributes. You're intelligent, kind, and very attractive."

"I'll make some simple man happy one day, but I'm in no rush to get married." She lowered herself onto a chair and pulled out a few papers from her knapsack.

"You needn't be in any hurry, but this pageant would be the perfect opportunity for you to meet some eligible men."

Katie blushed again. She reached out to grab his hand, which she gently kissed. "You're very kind to me. Thank you."

Resting his other hand on her head, Michael kissed her forehead. "You deserve the best, my dear."

Katie smiled. Changing the subject, she said, "What would you like for dinner?"

They moved into the kitchen where Michael held up a brown paper package. "I've brought home some sirloin steaks. They were left over from today."

"That's great. I'll cook them right away." She accepted the package from Michael and prepared the meal.

Michael left the kitchen and wandered over to his favourite chair. He leaned back and put up the recliner's foot rest. He raised his hands above his head and pointed his toes, stretching out his whole body. After he was relaxed, he considered ways to encourage Katie to enter the pageant.

Because of his previous association with the president, it might be possible for Katie to meet him. He wanted the best for her, which meant marrying the president whom Michael respected. He believed Katie would make him a good wife.

While eating dinner, Michael brought up the subject again. "Wouldn't you like to go?"

"I'd feel out of place." Katie concentrated on cutting up her steak into small, edible portions.

"You *have* to go." Michael pointed his fork in the air.

"Why?" Katie seemed surprised at his vehemence.

"You have to accept every opportunity." He speared a steamed green bean and brought it to his mouth.

"You're right." She raised her head and looked at him.

"You never know what will happen." Michael stuck his fork into the mashed potatoes and enjoyed their garlicky taste.

"I'll think about it," was all she said.

After they finished their meal, Katie cleared the dining table of the dirty dishes, and Michael helped carry them into the kitchen. She placed everything in the dishwasher, turned it on, and put the leftover food in the refrigerator. Michael left the kitchen and wandered into the living room.

He turned on his computer and searched popular ball gowns. He had helped his wife choose their daughters' dresses at times. He felt capable of finding something special for Katie.

He then googled dress stores and searched different sites. He noticed Woodiers was having a sale and perused their clothes. They had a variety of choices. He clicked on a long, sleek black dress. He would have to ask Katie for her size. He liked the dress and printed off a picture. He considered a few other possible ideas and printed them off as well.

He rose from the computer table and walked over to Katie who was sitting at the kitchen table. Books and papers were spread out all over. He tossed the pictures onto the books in front of her.

"What's this?" she asked. She picked up the papers and flipped through them.

"They're your new clothes for the beauty pageant." Michael stood in front of her.

"I'm not that attractive. I'd never win." But she perused the pictures and stopped at the black dress. It would really look good on her.

"Yes, you are, and I'm taking you. And you'll meet the president."

Katie's eyes widened, and her cheeks turned red. "Why are you so sure?"

"He owes me a favour."

She had no idea what kind of connection her cousin would have with the president. "What kind of favour?"

"Don't you worry," he said, waving his hand in the air. "What size are you?"

Katie, a little overwhelmed, blushed again, and said, "I'm a two."

"I'm buying you an entire new wardrobe." Michael returned to his computer and to the store's site, where he picked out the clothes, filled in his credit card information, and paid for them. The dresses would be delivered by the end of the week.

Katie came to stand behind him. "There's one major problem."

"I'll help you with whatever it is." Michael turned off the computer and turned in his chair to face her.

"I'm really embarrassed about this." Her cheeks were quickly turning a bright shade of red.

"It can't be that bad." He put his hands on her arms.

She stared at the floor. After a few moments, she raised her eyes and said, "I don't know how to dance."

Michael smiled. "That's not such a big deal. I can teach you how to dance. It's not that hard."

He rose from his chair with her hands in his and pulled her towards the middle of the room. He placed her right hand in his, her left hand on his waist, he slipped one arm around her back, and clasped her other hand.

Humming, Michael moved her about the floor. She stumbled at times and, occasionally, stepped on his foot.

"Like this," he said, "One...Two...Three, One...Two...Three." They twirled about the room. "Are you ready for some music?"

Katie nodded, and Michael turned on the radio. The station played a waltz. He returned to her, and she rested her hands in his. They danced around the room until the music ended, then stood in the middle of the floor, waiting for the next piece. It was a faster song.

Michael put his hands on his hips and said, "Let's see what you can do."

Katie listened to the music before she started moving. It took a little time for her body to sway, but she soon got the hang of it. Her gentle nature came out, along with her good sense of rhythm.

Then another slow song came on the radio. Michael and Katie paired up again and moved about, following with the music. She was a fast learner.

"You're ready." He smiled as she glided about the room. She floated as if her feet never touched the ground.

Chapter Thirteen

It was that day in August when Baltia was ready to put on a show and hold the president's beauty pageant and victory ball. The pageant would be held in the Ascurra Concert Hall, where the country's philharmonic orchestra held their concerts. It could boast an audience of 2,000 people. The pageant was also being televised around the world. So much was at stake, and everyone was excited.

The hall had been decorated in the country's colours of yellow and white. Streamers hung from the ceiling and colourful paintings of attractive women were pinned to the walls. The stage was hidden behind a large black curtain.

After the security guards made one last pass around the venue, people were let into the auditorium. Though they quickly took their seats, the noise level was high because everyone was talking.

At precisely eight o'clock, the lights were lowered, and the audience quieted down. When everyone was settled, a single light appeared to illuminate David Rush and Elaine Simon, the hosts of the pageant. Both were handsomely dressed. David wore a black tuxedo with a green shirt and yellow tie. Elaine matched him in a tight green dress with yellow accents.

David spoke first. "Welcome, everyone, to the president's beauty pageant. Tonight, twenty single women from all over the country will compete for the prize of Miss Baltia."

"The women are backstage," continued Elaine. "And they are waiting to be presented to the judges and to you."

"Speaking of judges," said David. "Let me introduce them to you. Please help me welcome the head of police, Brett Holsen; our bronze medallist at the World Cup of skating, Anna Kesti; and the youngest general in Baltia's military, General Arthur Blackwood."

The audience clapped as the judges stood, turned around, and waved to them. Everyone smiled for the camera. When they returned to their chairs, the audience's attention moved back to the stage and the hosts.

"And now," began Elaine. "It's time to meet the women competing for the prize of Miss Baltia."

The dark curtains parted to reveal bright lights shining on twenty young women standing on gold platforms. The hosts moved to the side of the stage and introduced each woman as they walked towards the front of the stage. They stood still for a few minutes while being introduced. Each woman wore an exquisite evening gown.

"First, please welcome Miss Susan Newcomb," announced Elaine. "She's twenty years of age and presently studying nursing at Graton University. She volunteers at the senior centre and enjoys working with the elderly."

The audience clapped.

"Next is Miss Patricia Simmons," continued David. "She's twenty-one, and in her last year at Graton University studying architecture. From an early age, she loved to create little buildings out of any material she could find. She loves animals and has two dogs and a cat."

The audience clapped.

"This is Miss Andrea Crost," said Elaine. "She's twenty-four years of age and is presently employed as a social worker specializing with children suffering with mental illness. She loves children and hopes to change their lives."

A loud cheer rose from the audience after hearing these words. Such a selfless woman would make a good Miss Baltia.

"Next, please let me introduce twenty-three-year-old Miss Katie Soros," said David. "She teaches grade three at Graton Elementary School and enjoys encouraging children to achieve their dreams."

Hearing these words, Katie felt a little shy. Entering the contest had been her cousin's idea, but the possibility was too much fun to pass up. This was a great chance to meet people.

When David spoke her name, Katie walked as gracefully as possible to the front of the stage, stepped up to a small platform, and stood on the platform where she slowly moved in a circle. Though she stood straight, she tried not to appear too stiff. She then turned around and headed backstage with the other women.

Katie listened as the other contestants were introduced. She picked up a few words, but most of what David and Elaine said slipped through her mind. She concentrated more on staring out at the sea of people who were privately judging her. She gazed at the real judges and wondered what they were thinking. She watched as they made notes on pads of paper.

As soon as all the women had showed off, David and Elaine moved back to the centre of the stage.

David said, "Now the judges will ask each contestant a question. The women will be judged on how they answer each question."

When Katie arrived at the stage's wings, the women were escorted into a back room. When the door was closed, no sound could be heard. A man with a clipboard and headphones called out one woman at a time. That woman left the room, returned to centre stage, and was asked three questions.

Katie glanced around at all the good-looking women and almost laughed at how serious everyone appeared. They were obviously very nervous. She watched as women left the room until it was down to her and two others. She was next, and was prepared when the man at the door signalled her forward.

After leaving the silent room, the noise of clapping could be heard from the audience. The loud sound surprised her and took her breath away. A man escorted her to the stage. She glided out to the centre of the stage where David and Elaine stood.

As soon as she reached her appointed spot, Elaine said, "Please welcome Miss Katie Soros."

The audience clapped.

Brett Holsen, the head of police, spoke first: "Hello, Miss Soros. My question for you is, if you could live anywhere in the world, where would it be and why?"

David handed Katie a microphone. She held it up to her mouth and said, "I wouldn't live anywhere else but here in Baltia. I'm very proud to be Baltian. This is a great country and we have everything we need. This is my home."

The audience applauded.

Next Anna Kesti spoke: "My question is, where would you like to be in five years?"

After taking a deep breath, Katie replied, "My dream is to help children achieve their dreams;

whatever they may be. I also hope to be married with a house full of children."

The audience applauded.

"My question is," asked General Arthur Blackwood. "If you won a million Euros, what would you do with the money?"

Katie smiled. "I would invest a small portion and give the rest to charities, such as Children with Autism and The Children's Mental Health Association."

The audience applauded.

"Thank you," said David. "Please go and stand with the other young ladies." He waved his right arm in the direction of the other contestants.

Katie smiled, showing off her shiny white teeth, and sauntered to the back of the stage.

After the last two ladies answered the judges' questions, and when all the contestants were standing on the stage, David announced, "Now the judges will be moved to a private room where they can compare notes and choose a winner."

"In the meantime," continued Elaine, "please enjoy the vocal stylings of Blaine West and his band, Doggy Park."

As Katie and the other women were moved off the stage and back into the silent room, the band set up and played their hit songs. Since they were the hottest band in the country, everyone enjoyed hearing their music and danced in their seats.

Though there was very little furniture in the silent room, there were some chairs around the circumference. Along one wall, there were two tables, one with bottles of juice and water, and the other with trays of fruit and cold vegetables. Assorted spinach and guacamole dips were also placed on the tables. Some of the women partook of the feast, but most were too nervous to eat.

Katie looked about the room and noticed three interesting women standing together. She liked their appearances so she approached them.

Susan introduced herself first. "Don't you find this just so exciting?"

The women glanced at each other and laughed, enjoying the moment.

"It's like being at the most important interview of your life," Patricia said as she adjusted her bra strap.

"Yes, for sure," agreed Andrea. She enjoyed turning left and right because her dress would flicker in the light. It was very pretty.

"I'm so nervous," admitted Susan. "You don't look nervous at all, Katie, but you must be."

"I am. My smile feels stuck to my face," confessed Katie, and the girls laughed.

"So, this is really going to be decided by those interview questions?" asked Patricia.

"Yes," said Andrea.

"I think I did well," Patricia continued. "But I really don't know."

Andrea patted Patricia on the arm. "As long as you did your best, you have nothing to worry about."

"I think I did." Patricia nodded, covering Andrea's hand with her own and squeezing it in thanks.

"I think I did, too," said Andrea.

"We all did." Susan smiled warmly. Her nervousness showed by her continuously sliding her hands down her dress as if to flatten it. "I just don't know how they are going to choose."

"I wish I knew the answer, too," agreed Patricia.

Katie rubbed her tummy. "I'm hungry."

She led her small group over to the food tables. The girls picked some fruit, cheese, and crackers and carried their plates to the chairs placed about the room.

Patricia looked around the room, taking in all the women. "Do you think you have a chance?"

Andrea munched on some grapes. "We've all got a chance."

"How do you feel about becoming the president's wife?" asked Susan. She placed a piece of cheese on a cracker and halved it in one bite.

The women inhaled deeply and slowly let out their breath. They watched each other, daring the other to respond.

Patricia spoke first. "I'd accept any proposal from him."

Susan talked behind her hand. "Me too."

"I'd marry him," admitted Andrea. She speared a strawberry and seemed to enjoy its sweetness based on her smile.

"Would you?" Susan asked Katie.

Katie shrugged her shoulders. "Perhaps."

"Are you kidding?" exclaimed Patricia. "He's gorgeous. Who wouldn't marry him?" She didn't expect anyone to disagree with her.

"But remember you'd be the first lady, too," Andrea whispered. She tried a few slices of melon.

"That's true." Susan put a hand over her heart.

The girls laughed, realizing what was before them. Each succumbed to their own thoughts as they nibbled on their snacks.

Suddenly, the room's door opened and the man with the headphones and clipboard entered the room. "Okay, ladies. A decision has been made. Please come up to the stage."

Chapter Fourteen

The concert hall resonated with the clamour of clapping. Some of the audience shouted or whistled when it was announced a decision had been made. Many took out their cell phones to record the exciting moment.

Unbeknownst to the crowd, the pageant contestants had lined up in the middle of the stage behind the black curtain. The women patted down their hair and arranged their evening gowns, hoping to look perfect. Each one had a strained smile resting on their lips.

Katie caught Susan's eye and they smiled at each other. They would soon know who had won. When Michael had first mentioned the contest to her, she didn't think she had a chance, but she was proud of how she had represented herself.

She considered the words of her fellow contestants. Would winning really mean becoming the president's wife? Though she had never met him, she had seen him many times on television. Shrugging her shoulders, she admitted to herself he was handsome. He had also done so much good for the country. Being his wife would be a great honour.

There was so much she could do if she were the president's wife. She could help children in a way she could never have done on her own. If she married the president, she would surely have good-looking, intelligent children.

She couldn't see the hosts, but based on the sounds from the audience, Katie assumed David and

Elaine had moved to centre stage in front of the curtain. She heard the clapping die down.

David said, "Let's open the curtain and reveal our contestants."

The huge, black curtain parted and drifted across the floor into the wings. The twenty single women stood showing off their best side. The array of colours reminded everyone of a rainbow.

The audience applauded and cheered.

Elaine said, "Everyone, please, let's welcome back our judges."

Katie watched as the three judges walked into the auditorium, waving at the crowd before taking their seats. Loud clapping resounded in the hall.

David held up his hands and the noise died down. He said, "Judges, may we please have the results?"

The man with the headphones and clipboard stood waiting in the wings with the envelope. Elaine sauntered over to him and he placed it in her hand. Elaine returned to centre stage, smiled at the crowd, and then opened the envelope. She pulled out a piece of paper, which she handed to David.

"We'll now announce the top four ladies," said David, reading from the paper. "They are Miss Andrea Crost, Miss Susan Newcomb, Miss Katie Soros, and Miss Patricia Simmons. Ladies, please come forward."

The audience clapped as the women moved to the front of the stage. They all appeared a little stunned at having their names called. They smiled at each other then joined hands.

"Drum roll, please," said David, still holding the piece of paper. "And the winner of the president's pageant is ... Miss Katie Soros."

Katie blushed. Andrea and Patricia, standing beside her, hugged her then pushed her forward. She couldn't remember how to walk and willed her feet to move. She walked over to stand beside the hosts. Elaine put a yellow satin sash around her with the words "Miss Baltia" written on it. David handed her the most exquisite bouquet of red roses she had ever seen.

Then Elaine and David took a few steps back and moved to the left side of the stage while the audience shouted congratulations. They had risen from their seats and were clapping loudly for the judges' choice.

Katie whispered to herself as she stood there. She reminded herself to breathe and just to stand straight and proud. A wide smile played on her face and her eyes sparkled, even though she almost fainted from the realization she had won. Her life was about to change.

From the side of the stage, Elaine said, "Let's congratulate all of the other contestants for their participation." She waved her hand in the direction of the women standing on the stage.

The audience applauded.

David put up his hand to quiet the crowd. Above the noise, he shouted, "I hope everyone will join us for the victory ball. Come and meet all our contestants."

David held out his arm, and Elaine took it in hers. They waved goodbye as they left the stage.

A handsome, young man in a black suit appeared at Katie's side and held out his right arm. She realized she was supposed to rest her hand there as he escorted her off the stage. As soon as the curtain closed, all the contestants came running up to Katie.

"Congratulations!" said Susan warmly, as she gave Katie a big hug.

"Yes, congratulations," Andrea said, rushing towards Katie.

Patricia touched Katie's arm. "We're so happy for you."

All the other women passed in front of Katie and offered their congratulations.

Handsome young men arrived and offered to escort them to the ball, taking place at the King August Hotel across the street. The women smiled sweetly at their partners. They raised their dresses with their right hand to make walking easier and followed their partners out of the building.

As the couples exited the main doors of the concert hall, there was a strong wind blowing and they were thrown about a bit as they walked across the street. It was dusk, and a full moon shone low in the sky.

The handsome men put their arms around their partners' waists and guided them through the wind. The women were glad when they reached the hotel's doors. A man in livery opened the doors for them.

Katie's mind was whirling. She had won the pageant, and now she would be introduced to the president. Would she like him? Would she be attracted to him? She couldn't wait to find out the answers to her many questions.

This was her first time in the King August Hotel and she marvelled at its finery. The lobby mirrors reflected rays of moonlight into the room, lighting her path. Her escort guided her along a red-carpeted passageway with walls boasting portraits of all the famous people who had stayed at the hotel. Katie tried to name their clients as she passed by the pictures.

They arrived at an ornate dressing room with mirrors along one side of the room above tables spread with makeup, brushes, and anything a woman would need. The handsome young men left the women alone, and Katie was glad for the respite. She had to compose herself before she met the president.

Once the last man had left and the door was closed, Patricia, Susan, and Andrea ran up to Katie.

"We're all as jealous as hell," Patricia admitted. "But we're so happy for you."

"Yes, we are," Andrea said while hugging Katie.

"I can't believe it," Katie murmured. "Everything is moving so fast."

Susan held out her arms for Katie, and they hugged. Katie enjoyed her strength. She had made a couple of friends since moving to Graton, but she was glad for some new ones with whom she could share this experience.

But she couldn't get it through her head she had won. She had hoped to win, but she had thought maybe her rustic background would disqualify her for the role of first lady. Yet, she had won, and she would be the night's centre of attention.

That scared her a bit, but she would prove the judges' decision had been the correct one. And when she met the president, she would do her best to charm him. This was her singular opportunity and she planned to take every advantage of it.

The women fidgeted over each other's gowns and helped style each other's hair. When they were finally presentable, the handsome, young men returned to the room to escort them into the ball.

Katie had to keep reminding herself to breathe as she was led into a huge ballroom where hundreds of people mingled. As the women arrived, the crowd parted and moved back towards the four walls. The young men gracefully led Katie and the other women into the centre of the room.

The orchestra played Baltia's national anthem, and everyone stood still and sang to the music.

As Katie sang, she allowed her eyes to tour the room. Everyone was dressed so attractively in tuxedos and flowing gowns. It was certainly a grand sight to see. She tried to spy the president, but she couldn't find him. *He must be here somewhere.*

After the national anthem, the orchestra played a waltz. Three well-dressed young men came up and took the hands of Andrea, Susan, and Patricia. The three women seemed to know the men because they immediately began conversing.

Katie stood in the middle of the room wondering what had happened. Would no one dance with her?

From across the room, Katie noticed the crowd part. The most attractive man she had ever seen strode confidently up to her, lifted her hand, and led her onto the dance floor.

"Congratulations, my dear," said the president as he twirled Katie around the room.

Katie felt dizzy. "Thank you."

Thomas slid his arm around her and held her tight. He slowed the pace and guided her to the left where they had more dance space, and were partially obscured by the other dancers.

The first thing she noticed about him was how good he smelled. There was something exquisite in that scent. She rested his cheek against his shoulder and inhaled. She felt very secure in his strong arms, and she loved the way his amazing blue eyes would stare right into hers.

"I reviewed your biography, as I did with the other ladies," Thomas said with a big smile on his face.

"Did you have a favourite?" Katie smiled back.

"No. I decided to leave that to the judges. I trusted their opinions." Thomas adjusted to the new music, which had a faster tempo.

"And how do you feel about the result?" Katie couldn't help turning her face away, hoping to hide the blush.

"I'm very pleased."

Katie turned back, gazed into his eyes, and knew he spoke the truth. She peered around and noticed everyone was dancing. She could just relax in this man's arms and hope it led to something that could change her life.

"Are you tired?" Thomas asked, and he slowed the pace.

"Yes. I am a little. It's been a hectic day." She leaned into his chest.

Thomas danced her off the floor to where some chairs were placed against the wall. A couple were vacant, and Katie thankfully fell into one. After she arranged her dress around her legs, she lay back into the chair and sighed.

"I'm so glad to sit. Thank you. Would you mind finding me something to drink?" Katie put a hand to her throat.

Thomas raised a finger, and a waiter magically appeared with two glasses of champagne. The waiter lowered the tray to Thomas, and he lifted the glasses off the tray and handed one to Katie.

Thankful for the liquid, Katie took a few small sips. She could have finished the glass in one gulp, but that wouldn't be very ladylike. She breathed deeply.

"Feel better?" asked Thomas.

"Much better. Thank you." Katie widened her smile, hoping to prove how grateful she was.

"Now let me get it straight," began Thomas. "You used to live in the country, and you lost your parents. I'm sorry."

Katie nodded her thanks.

"You teach grade three and you love children."

Again, she nodded.

"And you would like children of your own?" This question was in the forefront of his mind.

Katie blushed and smiled. She gazed into his eyes and said, "Yes. Very much."

Thomas heaved a noticeable sigh of relief. Katie let out a quick laugh when she realized the importance of the question. Everyone always wondered why the president didn't have any children.

"How do you feel about politics?"

"I understand them, but it's not a major interest for me. I have no doubt you're running the country in the best possible way. I'd rather leave the politics to you."

Thomas seemed pleased with her answer. "How would you feel about meeting great men and women from all over the world?"

"I'd be honoured. I have no prejudice. To me, everyone is equal," Katie said as she clasped her hands in her lap.

Thomas finished his champagne and delicately removed her empty glass from her hand. He placed them on a waiter's tray and reached out for two full glasses. After he had passed one to Katie, he asked, "Do you have any questions for me?"

She was again grateful for the champagne, providing her with some strength and courage. "Why did you hold the pageant?"

Thomas smirked. "I thought this would be the best way to find Baltia's new first lady."

"And now I've won. What do you plan to do with me?" Katie couldn't believe she had said that. It came out faster than she expected, but she needed that question answered.

"I plan on marrying you," Thomas replied, slowly enunciating each word.

"Is that a proposal?" Katie was surprised.

"Yes."

Katie peered around the room. No one could overhear their conversation. "Don't tell me you've got the ring on you?"

Thomas laughed. "Actually, I do." He rummaged in the breast inside pocket of his jacket and pulled out a ring box. He got down on one knee.

Though the crowd had given the couple some privacy, they all turned to watch the president propose.

"I know this is a little fast, but why should we wait? I will love you more than life itself. I will be there for you whenever you need me through sickness and in health. If you agree to be my wife, you will make me the happiest man on earth."

Katie gazed at the ring and smiled. It was gorgeous. A single large diamond surrounded by smaller white diamonds.

"Would you marry me, Katie Soros?" asked Thomas, holding up the ring.

She smiled and simply answered, "Yes."

Thomas threw his arms around her and gave her a long, deep kiss as the crowd cheered. The couple waved, and then returned to their seats. Everyone was obviously thrilled about their engagement.

Katie's eyes brightened as she noticed someone coming towards them. Just as Thomas was about to speak, Katie stood up and welcomed an older man into her arms.

"I've been wondering where you were," Katie said to the man. Then to Thomas, she added, "I'd like to introduce my cousin, Michael, at whose house I've been living."

"I hope I'm not interrupting anything," Michael apologized.

"No, please don't worry," Thomas reassured him as he held out his hand, which Michael shook.

"Thank you, Mr. President," said Michael. "And congratulations on your engagement to my cousin."

"Do we know each other?" Thomas asked. He was looking strangely at Michael.

"Yes, sir. We met a few months ago."

"I'm having trouble placing you. Could you please remind me?"

Michael stared at the people milling around them. Once he was assured they couldn't be overheard, he whispered, "The assassination."

"Yes, yes, right. You're Michael Soros. How are you doing?"

"Very well, thank you, sir." Michael's face brightened. He looked happy the president had recognized him.

"I still owe you a favour," Thomas remembered as he rested his right hand on Michael's shoulder.

"I was going to ask you to take my cousin's hand in marriage." Michael picked up Katie's hand and squeezed it.

"Way ahead of you, sir," Thomas replied as he, Michael, and Katie burst out laughing.

Michael peered at Katie and understood from her smile she was very happy.

"I should ask for your blessing." Thomas put out his hand for Michael to shake.

Michael said, "But, of course, Mr. President. You have my full approval."

"So, I still owe you a favour," Thomas pointed out.

"Yes, I guess so, Mr. President."

"Call me Thomas. If you're ever in need anything, do not hesitate to contact me."

"Thank you very much ... Thomas."

Thomas rested his hand on Michael's shoulder before reaching out for Katie. He drew her to him, and held her tightly as he guided her onto the dance floor. She glanced back and waved at her cousin before she was swept away.

Chapter Fifteen

One man attending the ball was not enjoying himself. Harmon stood against the wall, totally absorbed in his own thoughts. As people passed, they shook his hand and bowed their heads to him, but he barely acknowledged them. He was feeling sad and depressed because he hadn't heard from Leah.

Since her separation from Thomas, Leah had not contacted him. She didn't tell him where she was going, causing him much distress. He had called every place he could think of, but no one could give him any information.

Leah's betrayal consumed him. He had deluded himself that she would move in with him. He did love her more than she loved him but, if she moved in with him, it would be a slap in Thomas's face. Harmon thought she might want to get back at Thomas.

But she didn't move in, and now he had no idea how to find her. He had never taken much interest in her life, so he didn't know any of her friends, but he still hoped she would contact him. He would often check his email and phone, but there was no message from her.

Harmon remembered the great sex with Leah. They had understood each other's wants and needs. And, it had been regular affair; Leah had come to his house two to three times a week. Not only was his heart broken, he was frustrated.

He had never gone so long without sex. It was a position he didn't think he'd ever be in. As he searched the room, his glance fell on many lovely women. He wasn't prepared to give up his feelings for Leah, but he needed sex. Given his position as vice-president, he was sure any woman would go home with him.

But he had to be careful. If a woman revealed their intimate moments, that could jeopardize his relationship with Leah. She would definitely not come back to him if she heard he had been with other women.

Again, he screened the women in the ballroom, searching for one who would entice his sexual desires. He spotted one brown-haired beauty dressed in a tight blue dress. She stood just off the dance floor with another woman.

He watched her for a few minutes before he decided to introduce himself and invite her to dance. He had no doubt she would agree. No woman would turn him down if she knew what was good for her.

As he crossed the floor, he kept his head held high as everyone shook his hand while bowing to him. He enjoyed and expected this amount of respect. His position as vice-president demanded such attention.

Then he came alongside a man whose back was to him. As the man turned around, he stared Harmon straight in the eye. Harmon offered his right hand.

Harmon asked, "Aren't you going to shake my hand?"

"No," said the man.

"Everyone must shake my hand and bow to me," Harmon snarled menacingly.

"Well, this man won't." The man's rigid posture stood unyielding.

Harmon was furious. His face reddened, and his chest swelled. He shouted, "How dare you. Bow to me!"

"No." The man turned his back on Harmon and walked away.

Harmon grabbed the waiter who stood near him. "Do you know that man?"

The waiter quivered in his shoes while Harmon clutched the lapel of his black jacket.

"That's the butcher, sir," the waiter whispered as he balanced his tray.

Harmon stared at the waiter. "The butcher? Are you sure? What's his name?"

"Michael Soros, sir."

Harmon wondered if he was related to Katie Soros. "What do you know about him?"

The nervous waiter glanced at the people around them. He was fearful of being overheard. "Well, sir, he's a widower, and a well-liked man."

"Really? Well, he'll suffer for his disrespect," Harmon growled, clenching his fists.

The waiter steadied his tray and quickly moved away from Harmon. He ran across the room, putting distance between them.

The brown-haired woman in the corner no longer held any interest for Harmon. He raged over the insult and stomped loudly about the ballroom. He was so furious he was afraid he would hit someone, so he decided to leave the ball before he did something he would regret.

He stomped to his car, yanked open the door, threw himself into the driver's seat, and banged his fists on the steering wheel. He had been humiliated. If Michael Soros could get away with such insolence, then maybe others would try.

He would have the man executed. As he considered the words for an execution order, he knew he had to make a strong case. Michael's insolence must not go unpunished. To Harmon, just the fact he didn't shake his hand or bow to him was a sufficient reason to have the man executed for treason.

Then it occurred to him: he would tell Thomas it was Michael who hired the assassins to kill him. That would be the perfect solution to his problem. The guards had stopped looking for the culprit after the assassins had been executed. The whole country knew the assassins did not reveal who had hired them.

Harmon was very pleased with himself. Driving home as quickly as possible, Harmon arrived in record time. He dashed into his home office and turned on his computer. He drafted an order for Michael Soros's execution.

Once the decree was written, he poured himself a large glass of whiskey. He put the glass to his lips and drank down the entire contents. As the strong liquor passed through his body, he felt himself begin to relax, but he was still mad. He would see that imbecile dead.

Chapter Sixteen

Thomas leaned back in his black leather chair, drinking scotch. He swirled the liquid and a couple of ice cubes around in the glass and then took a sip. He repeated this procedure a few times before drinking down the rest in his glass.

He seemed surprised when the glass was empty. Using one arm to raise himself, he pushed himself up straight and hobbled to the liquor cabinet. Picking up the bottle of scotch, he poured himself another glass. He stared at the empty bottle then shrugged his shoulders before returning to his chair.

What a night. He sighed loudly. It certainly had been eventful, and the beauty pageant was a triumph. He had enjoyed the women's parade, but he didn't have a favourite. He hadn't allowed himself to choose, fearing his choice and the judges' would differ.

The audience was obviously pleased with the decision. They gave Katie a standing ovation when her name was announced as the winner. She appeared humble and respectful yet pleased with the result. She had gazed into the crowd and had thanked everyone with a sweep of her hand, and she handled herself well when the centre of attention. The president's wife must fill that position often.

Wasn't it wonderful he had found a new wife so easily? Even though the pageant was Martin's idea, he hadn't been sure it would work out. He had a few sleepless nights worried the judges would choose someone who didn't appeal to him. He was greatly relieved they had chosen so well.

Thomas raised his arms behind his back, stretched out his legs, pointed his toes, and thought about Katie. She was definitely a very attractive woman with her long, curly brown hair and warm brown eyes. Those eyes had mesmerised him. Her skin was like porcelain and she wore her makeup well. He was pleased she didn't overdo it. Leah always wore too much makeup.

It had thrilled him the way Katie had moved across the stage. She was so graceful and had held herself with so much composure, only impressing Thomas more. And, he loved the way she fit into his arms as they danced.

Her sweet voice charmed him. Her words were lyrical as she articulated her thoughts. As they danced, they regaled each other with their dreams and passions, and they had so much in common. The fact that Katie was a teacher inspired Thomas. He admired teachers for their commitment to helping children. He remembered a few teachers from his past who had influenced his life.

Both agreed they should have children as soon as possible. Katie would make a wonderful mother, and he didn't want to wait. No children had been a major stress with Leah. A shiver ran down his spine just thinking of having children. He would love and support Katie as best as possible. He hoped their wedding night would bring about the conception of his son.

First thing in the morning, he made a note to his staff to call a decorator and completely overhaul the master bedroom. A fresh start was necessary. The room would be painted blue, a favourite colour of both Thomas and Katie.

There was a fantastic furniture store just outside of town that sold the most amazing natural oak furniture. He had always wanted pieces from their collection, but Leah didn't approve of wood. Nothing would please him more than to pick out what he wanted. He was sure Katie would approve.

Katie. Just thinking of her name made his heart race. What would sex be like with her? It had been too long since he had some good, loving sex. Sex with Leah had been a disappointment. He believed it would be different with Katie.

He texted Katie: "Available tonight?"

He didn't have to wait long for her reply.

"Yes, I'm free."

Pleased with her response, he wrote back, "I'll pick you up at 7."

"I'll be ready," was her reply.

A new Japanese restaurant had opened in town and they boasted curtained rooms where their patrons could enjoy a meal with some privacy. The newspaper just posted a review and they gave it top scores. Thomas booked a room and ordered their set dinner meal of appetizers and entrees for two.

During the day, he couldn't stop wondering about their dinner and how it would go. Would she be ready on time? He believed in being punctual. He was always early for all his appointments because he would rather wait for someone than have them wait for him.

Choosing what to wear gave Thomas some concern. He finally settled on a pair of black jeans and simple blue sweater. He was tired of dressing up all the time. When he came home from work, he preferred to jump into a sweatshirt and sweatpants. With Leah, it had been all about the clothes. With Katie, he could be more natural and relaxed. It would be the simple life for them—something he preferred.

Thomas arrived at Katie's house at ten to seven. He waited in his car with the radio playing the popular songs of the day. He turned down the volume and lowered the side window. He noticed one of the front curtains move. When the front door opened, Katie stood there dressed in a stylish but simple floral dress. The colours flattered her, and she gave off an aura of happy optimism.

He jumped out of the car and dashed towards her house. He was thrilled to see her, making him feel like a teenager again. A genuine smile of happiness lit up his face, giving away his feelings.

When he reached the porch, Katie walked towards him. He raised his arm and Katie slipped her arm in his. She was also smiling. Neither spoke because neither could express their joy in words at this moment.

Thomas opened the car door and assisted Katie into the front seat. He ran around the car to get into the driver's side. Once his seat belt was fastened, he winked at Katie and then turned on the engine. After looking for oncoming traffic, he moved out into the street. They drove for a few minutes without speaking.

Thomas glanced at Katie and said, "You look great."

"Thank you." Katie blushed. "You seem happy."

He noticed her eyes wander over his body. "Yes, I am. Haven't been this happy in ages and it's all thanks to you."

She turned sideways in her seat to look at him. "Me? Why me? We just met."

"You're everything I've always wanted. I've been blind." He glanced out his rear mirror before he made a right turn.

"And your blindness has gone?"

"Yes." He reached out and lightly grazed his fingers over hers until she took his hand in hers and held it tight.

Since the traffic was light, Thomas could watch her facial expressions while she looked out the front window. Her brown eyes were open wide and a smile played on her lips. Their destination was a secret and he hoped she liked surprises.

A few minutes later, they arrived at the Japanese restaurant. He parked the car in the rear parking lot. Katie waited until Thomas opened the car door for her. She slid out and into his arms. He gave her a quick kiss on the cheek then assisted her into the restaurant through a back door. A man waited just inside the doors to escort them to their private room.

"This is lovely," said Katie. "I read a few reviews about this place. Good choice for a first date."

"First date? Isn't this our second?" Thomas squirmed in his chair trying to get comfortable.

Katie held up a finger and replied, "No. We first met last night. That wasn't a date."

Thomas grinned. "That's true. Okay, this is our first date. And how would you like the date to proceed?"

"Let's eat, enjoy, talk, laugh, and hopefully build a good relationship."

"Brilliant. My wishes exactly." He reached out and touched Katie's hand lying on the table. She didn't remove her hand and allowed him to rest his there. It was the sweetest touch.

A waitress arrived carrying a slender white bottle containing hot sake, and two small white glasses, which she placed on the table. Using tongs, she gave both Thomas and Katie a small, hot, white cloth. When both had wiped their hands, the waitress took their cloths and laid them on her tray before she disappeared.

Thomas picked up the sake, poured Katie a glass, and then served himself. They held their glasses high in the air, clinked them together, and then they drank. Though Katie took a few small sips, Thomas emptied half the glass's content in one gulp.

The energy is the room sizzled though neither could express their happiness. They sat in silence until the waitress returned with two small bowls of miso soup. She placed the bowls in front of them and then asked, "Would you prefer spoons?"

Katie shook her head no. Thomas answered for the both of them. "We're fine, thanks."

After bowing her head, the waitress left the couple alone to enjoy the soup. It was hot and the couple drank it slowly from the small bowl. They couldn't stop smiling at each other.

Thomas picked up the sake and filled his cup. He topped Katie's glass and broke the silence. "Do you intend to continue teaching?"

She swirled the soup left over in her bowl and then drank it down. "Actually, I'd prefer to build a foundation for children with mental illnesses."

"Isn't there one?" Thomas sipped his sake. He had finished the soup and found it delicious.

"There are a few clinics, but I'd like to build a main facility here in Graton." She dabbed her mouth with her napkin.

"That's a great idea. It would provide for many jobs."

There was a vacant building over on Grey Street, just on the edge of the downtown but central enough to be available to anyone in need. He would instruct his staff to find a contracting firm to clean the place up. He could hire specialized doctors, nurses, and social workers to work in the centre. Hadn't he read something a few weeks ago about more jobs were needed for people in the medical profession? He made a mental note to check on that in the morning.

Thomas almost burst out laughing at Katie's expression when she said, "Can we do that?"

"Definitely. I'm already thinking about all the possibilities." He finished off the sake in his glass.

The waitress returned with two small bowls of salad and Agedashi tofu. She removed the miso bowls. Before she left, she asked, "More sake?"

Thomas nodded his head and the waitress left. He picked up the plate of tofu and held it for Katie. Using chopsticks, she removed a piece and placed it on the small plate in front of her. Thomas removed another with his chopsticks and popped it in his mouth. He enjoyed its savory flavour.

When he cleared his throat, Katie looked up. As she gazed into his eyes, he said, "Have you had many boyfriends?"

Katie played with her salad. "I've had a couple, but nothing serious."

"Are you a virgin?" He was a little embarrassed for speaking so bluntly. He glanced at Katie as she blushed.

After a moment, she whispered, "Yes, I am."

Thomas was truly surprised. This was a bonus. He patted her hand and said, "I promise to be gentle and I'll not push you. We'll go at your speed."

Katie gazed up into his eyes and smiled. "Could we wait until the honeymoon?"

He hesitated a second and then said, "Yes, of course." He picked up her hand and kissed it.

The couple giggled as the waitress appeared, removed the dirty dishes, and brought clean ones. Another waitress appeared with plates of shrimp and vegetable tempura, a dynamite roll, and tuna and salmon sashimi.

Thomas picked up a piece of the dynamite roll and dunked it in the soya sauce before placing it in his mouth. It tasted so good.

Katie rested her napkin on her lap, picked up her chopsticks, and then manoeuvred them around a piece of salmon sashimi. She dipped it in the soya sauce and then put it in her mouth. As she chewed, she smiled at him.

"I can't wait to try all the different foods in other countries," she confessed. She tried a sweet potato tempura and dipped it in the sauce.

He stopped chewing and swallowed. "You'll travel with me?"

"Of course. Where you go, I go."

"Leah stopped travelling with me years ago. I missed having the company at night when all the day's business had been concluded."

She put her hand over Thomas's and assured him, "I'll be the kind of wife you need."

He put down his chopsticks and covered her hand with his other hand and held on tight. "Music to my ears. I'll show you the world."

"I can't wait." She finished the dynamite roll.

The couple concentrated on the last pieces of the meal. Thomas thoroughly enjoyed the food and Katie appeared quite content. Their conversation continued easily. He felt very comfortable with her.

The waitress appeared and removed all the empty dishes. She left as silently as she arrived.

Katie laid her arms on the table, and Thomas laced his fingers with hers, as they looked into each other's eyes. Thomas felt emotions he had thought were gone forever. It was amazing how much this woman enticed him. He couldn't take his eyes off her and he ached to hold her.

The waitress returned. "Would you like some dessert?"

Thomas cocked his head, signing to Katie to make the final decision, and she answered, "No, thank you. I've had enough."

"Thank you. Just the cheque please."

The waitress nodded her head and left the room.

"What happens now?" Katie asked.

Staring into those sublime brown eyes, he replied, "What do you want to happen?"

Her eyes were open and honest. "I'd like to get married."

Thomas jumped up and moved around the table to sit beside her. "Then married we shall be. Would you like to set the date?"

Katie put her left hand on his shoulder and smiled. With her right hand, she pulled out her cell phone and turned to her calendar.

"How long should we wait?" she said, peering at her phone.

"I don't think we have to worry. The whole country expects us to marry. What about in three months? That will give us enough time to set everything up." He raised his finger and brushed it across her cheek.

Katie turned her head and kissed his finger. "Three months is good. May I meet with your staff? I would need their help."

"They'll do most of the work. Just tell them what you would like it. I trust you." He kept his finger on her lips and trailed his finger along them.

"Thank you. It will be simple but tasteful."

"Perfect. In three months, we wed." He placed his hand behind her head and gave her his most amorous kiss, making them both shake in their shoes. Their feelings were strong, and they couldn't wait to give into them.

Chapter Seventeen

It was two days after the pageant and Harmon still fumed about Michael's behaviour at the ball. He couldn't get the betrayal out of his mind. He replayed the scenario over and over, thinking of other ways he could have responded. He should have arrested him then and there, but he would get back at him when the execution decree was revealed.

Harmon glanced at his watch; it read half past seven. Thomas should be wrapping up his day by now. Harmon made his way to Thomas's office carrying a bottle of scotch.

He wanted nothing to stand in his way of executing the decree. Thomas was too kind to his citizens, so Harmon didn't think Thomas would approve of the decree if he was sober.

Thomas also did not appear to know he had planned the assassination. He hadn't been treating him any differently, and he had never said anything to him about the assassination. Harmon felt confident no one knew he had planned it.

Harmon knocked on Thomas's office door a couple of times before walking in. As expected, Thomas was alone, sitting behind his desk, working on his laptop. His desk was organized, as all the papers were in their appropriate trays.

"Like a drink?" Harmon asked as he held up the bottle of scotch.

Closing his laptop screen, Thomas rubbed his eyes then said, "Why not?"

Harmon smiled as he grabbed two glasses from a nearby table. He poured the alcohol into both glasses and then handed one to Thomas.

"Cheers," Harmon said, raising his glass.

"Cheers," answered Thomas. He touched his glass with Harmon's.

After taking a small sip, Harmon gazed over the edge of the glass at Thomas. He watched him finish off the scotch with two deep gulps.

"What did you say to the Japanese businessmen?" Harmon asked. He leaned over and filled Thomas's glass.

"The Japanese businessmen. Right, the Japanese businessmen. Told them we'd review their trade deal. We'll give them an answer by the end of the week," Thomas said. After glancing into his glass, he put it to his lips and took a deep sip.

Harmon watched Thomas's every movement. He tried to determine what kind of shape he was in and how much alcohol he would have to give him to get him drunk enough to sign the decree.

"Should we be doing business with them?" asked Harmon.

"Of course," Thomas replied. "Their business will be good for Baltia."

Harmon held up the bottle. "More?"

"Sure." Thomas leaned over to Harmon and held out his glass.

Harmon filled it, and then brought up another issue they were dealing with in government. He used his questions to help gauge Thomas's level of intoxication.

Harmon asked, "What about the new bridge?"

"It will be built. There will be some inconvenience for the people who used the old bridge, but the engineers promised not to take longer than a month." Thomas slouched in his chair.

"That's good." Harmon took another small sip. He wanted Thomas to think he was getting drunk, too.

Thomas stared into the bottom of his empty glass. "Yeah, we got a good deal on the steel, so the bridge will come in under budget."

"That's always good." Harmon noticed Thomas's empty glass but waited to refill it.

Thomas's hand wobbled as he picked up a piece of paper on his desk and passed it to Harmon. "The newspaper got wind of the bridge. There'll be a story in tomorrow's issue."

"Good," Harmon said. He felt Thomas had waited long enough. "More scotch?"

"Yes, please." Thomas held out his glass and tried to keep it steady.

Testing the president, Harmon asked, "Have you heard from Leah?"

"Leah? Nope. She's gone for good." Thomas shook his head and stuck out his tongue in disgust.

"Gone where?" Harmon found himself shaking nervously.

"I don't know. Some friend's condo. Oh, wait, she left that place. Moved to ... can't remember." Thomas took a sip then licked his lips.

Harmon was excited. He hoped when Thomas was drunk enough, he would betray Leah's location. "Is it somewhere in Baltia?"

"What somewhere? Oh, Leah. Yeah, she still has a few shallow friends left."

Harmon kept up with the questions, hoping Thomas would reveal something. "Has she taken all her belongings?"

"Yeah, I guess she did." Thomas yawned, but Harmon didn't know if it was from boredom or he was just tired.

He decided to push him further. "Where did she take them?"

Thomas got angry. "What do you care?"

"I'm just worried about her." But Harmon was afraid he had gone too far.

"What's there to worry about? She's gone. Good riddance." Thomas drank down the rest of his scotch and then held out his glass.

Harmon quickly poured more scotch. "You feel nothing for her?"

Thomas spat out the words, "Nothing at all."

Harmon was disappointed with Thomas's responses, but he didn't want to anger him any further. He needed him for something more important.

Thomas interrupted Harmon's thoughts. "Let's have one more glass and then I'm going home."

"Okay, one more." Harmon was glad for a reason to give him more alcohol.

Thomas took a sip, burped, then said, "Good scotch."

"Thanks."

"Where'd you get it?" Thomas held his glass in the air and peered through the alcohol at the light in the ceiling.

"From that Scottish guy, Ian McMaster." Harmon held up the empty bottle for Thomas to examine.

"He gets that for you?" Thomas asked. "I didn't realize you two were such good friends."

Harmon shrugged his shoulders. "He helps me out from time to time."

"Oh, by the way," said Thomas. He opened his mouth wide, attempting to enunciate his words. "I'm going to Paris tomorrow for a couple of days."

"To meet with the French president about our new trade deal?"

Thomas burped the word, "Yes."

"Is Katie going with you?"

"Yes," muttered Thomas. "I'm going to expose her to French cuisine."

"Sounds like a good trip then."

"Should be."

"I'll take care of everything while you're away." Harmon gave Thomas a wide smile, hoping to convey confidence.

Thomas frowned. He looked like he was going to say something, but no words left his mouth.

After a few moments, Thomas held up his hand and said, "Well, this has been fun, but I should go home."

Thomas had trouble rising from his chair. He sank back in it to recover. He tried again, and this time, he succeeded. He rose, placed his empty glass on the table, and tried to stand straight.

Harmon stuck out his hand to stop his movement. "There's actually another matter I'd like to discuss with you."

Thomas waved his arms in the air, emphasizing his displeasure at that statement. "Not now, Harmon. I'm too drunk. I'm going home."

"Just one more thing?" Harmon begged.

Thomas stomped his foot. "Damn it all, man. What is it?"

Feeling the time was right, Harmon said, "I have a decree I need for you to approve before I take it before the cabinet."

"Decree for what?" Thomas accepted the paper Harmon handed him.

"The decree is for the execution of a traitor." Harmon articulated his words.

Thomas tried to read but paper but couldn't focus on the words. Harmon wondered if Thomas could read it. He kept moving the paper closer to his eyes and then away. "Treason? Who? That's terrible."

"This man is arrogant and audacious. He's the one who organized your assassination," said Harmon, attempting to pour gas on the fire. "We have to get rid of him before he destroys us."

Thomas shook his head and just stared at Harmon for a few minutes. Then, in frustration, Thomas threw it down the table. "I'll deal with this when I return from France."

Harmon picked up the paper and handed it back to Thomas. "No. We have to deal with it now."

"When is the execution scheduled for?"

Harmon noticed a backgammon set sitting on a bookshelf. He picked it up and opened it. He took out the dice and rolled them on the desk. They showed the number three.

"He will be executed on the thirteenth of March."

"Then we have time." Thomas tried to cross the floor, but his limbs wouldn't participate. He moved back to his couch and plopped down.

Harmon was furious at himself for getting the president so drunk. He wouldn't read the decree now, so Harmon grabbed a pen off his desk and forged Thomas's signature. He would take it before the cabinet while Thomas was away. He should be able to arouse the anger of the ministers if he told them it was Michael who planned the assassination.

Thomas let out a deep sigh. "I'm going to lie down for a minute. Let yourself out." Thomas put his head on the cushion and he was out.

Harmon went over and waved his hand in front of Thomas's eyes, but Thomas didn't move. He then let out a loud snore. He was out cold and probably wouldn't even remember tonight.

Harmon ran to his office and put the signed decree into his vault. He would give Michael Soros a few months of freedom until the decree would be made public.

His anger towards Michael was stronger than ever, especially now he had this decree. But his thoughts returned to Leah. He had hoped when he got Thomas drunk, Thomas would reveal Leah's location, but that plan had failed. He would just have to continue to wait to hear from her.

~

The next morning, after Thomas and Katie had left for France, Harmon entered the cabinet meeting and stood before the ministers.

Harmon held the decree high and announced, "This man planned the president's assassination."

The ministers shouted their approval for Michael's execution.

Chapter Eighteen

Three months passed, and the day for the Thomas's and Katie's wedding had arrived. The country had talked about nothing else for the last few weeks. Everyone was invited since it was taking place in Graton's main state park. It was Thomas's intention to have the biggest party ever.

The whole park was decorated with white streamers draped through the beech and elm trees; pots of white roses, white carnations, and white chrysanthemums were arranged throughout the wedding area. A considerable number of sturdy wooden chairs were set up; each chair was covered with a white cloth. A trail of white satin led to a stage where the ceremony would be performed. A white flowered trellis stood where the couple would stand.

Thomas's first thought upon waking was of Katie. They had strolled around the dark, silent park the night before, checking on what had been prepared for them. The sight of all the chairs amazed them, as well as the numerous vases of white flowers. The aroma from all the flowers was so strong the couple felt they were floating on the scent. Both approved of the decorations.

During their stroll, Katie held tightly to Thomas's hand. Their feelings were strong, which amazed them both since they had only been together for such a short time. They had been meeting almost daily, and they had enjoyed their few days in Paris, where they visited many romantic sights.

After a long tour around the park, Thomas drove Katie to the King August Hotel, where he had arranged for her to spend the night. He had filled the suite with red roses and jugs of iced tea, one of Katie's favourites. He also hired people to help her dress and do her hair and makeup in the morning. He didn't want her to worry about a thing.

In the morning, Thomas had a leisurely breakfast while reading the newspaper. Since he had nowhere to go and nothing to do, he didn't know what to do with himself. He paced the halls, finding himself in the library where he perused the novels, looking for something to read. A large number of books rested on shelves covering the walls of the room. After looking through them, he decided he didn't feel much like reading.

He ended up in front of a bookcase holding all the blue-ray movies. He read through a few titles until he found one starring Drew Barrymore. She was one of Katie's favourite actresses. He picked up *Ever After: A Cinderella Story,* put it in the machine, and turned on the television.

He noticed some similarities between the movie and his life. Drew's character, Danielle, resembled Katie in some ways. Katie was an orphan, too, and more a country girl than a city one. The love and passion he felt for her were similar to the prince's affections for Danielle. Thomas's and Katie's ending would be the same: they would marry and live happily ever after.

Just as the movie ended, Arthur, the butler, knocked at the open door. "Sir, it's time you dressed."

"That time already?" Thomas stood up, stretched, and then headed out of the library. The wedding was scheduled for one o'clock in the afternoon, so everyone would have the whole day and night to celebrate.

Arthur interrupted Thomas's thoughts, "I laid out your tuxedo on your bed."

"Thank you, Arthur."

As he passed by him, Thomas patted Arthur on the shoulder, then headed up the stairs to his bedroom. He took some time dressing, making sure everything was perfect. After adjusting his tie and combing his hair, he was ready. He strolled down the stairs, out the front door, and into a waiting limousine.

When Thomas arrived at the park, he marvelled at the decorations in the daylight. The sweet aroma of all the flowers still wafted in the air. It was wonderful to see the number of guests, and he was glad he would be able to share his happiness with the world. He peered out into the crowd and recognized most of the spectators. A lot of dignitaries settled in the front seats. Behind them were the Baltians. The wedding had brought together a grand assortment of people.

While Thomas strode up the path to the stage, the twenty-piece orchestra were playing excerpts from Mozart's *The Marriage of Figaro*. The songs blended nicely with the occasion because of the romantic tone of the music.

When he reached his appointed position on the stage, Thomas waited impatiently for the music to change to the wedding march. He couldn't wait to see his bride. It felt like Mexican jumping beans were exploding throughout his body.

The orchestra ended the Mozart piece and the people went silent. Just when everyone thought they were going to burst, the conductor tapped the music stand and they played *Le Cygne* (The Swan) by Saint-Saens, a favourite of Katie's.

First to appear up the aisle was Anna, Thomas's seven-year-old niece, wearing an adorable pink fluffy dress. Obviously excited, she pranced down the aisle. She carried a small basket of white flower petals, which she dropped from time to time. She giggled and waved to Thomas before disappearing into the front pew beside her mother and father.

Next to appear were three bridesmaids, dressed in attractive, light blue dresses cut to fit them perfectly. Katie had asked Andrea, Patricia, and Susan to be her bridesmaids since they had become such good friends after the pageant. The three women had readily agreed.

After the bridesmaids, the matron-of-honour walked down the aisle. Helen was Katie's best friend since childhood and they had shared many special moments together. Katie had been Helen's maid-of-honour at her wedding. Helen wore a simple, yet tasteful, dark blue dress.

The orchestra allowed the last notes of the music to die off before beginning the wedding march. Thomas stared down the aisle and saw the most beautiful thing he had ever seen in his whole life.

Katie appeared wearing a long, white lace dress and veil. The bodice was tight around her slender body and there was just a wisp of a sleeve. The dress flowed to the ground with a three-foot train. Her sheer veil covered her face, which Thomas saw more clearly as she floated towards him.

When Katie reached his side, Thomas inhaled deeply, in awe of such magnificence. As the minister spoke, he barely heard the words. All he could focus upon was the angel beside him. He stood still, staring into his bride's deep brown eyes.

As the minister droned on, Thomas glanced at him from time to time. He heard Katie repeat her name, and then the minister said his name. Thomas continued to stare at his bride.

Thomas noticed the minister had stopped talking and was staring at him. He realized he had to say, "I do."

After Katie spoke those words, Thomas gathered her into his arms and kissed her with all the passion he could show. Katie was left breathless. A great cheer rose from the audience when the couple turned to face them. Everyone stood and clapped loudly.

After the newlyweds waved at the crowd, Thomas pulled Katie closer and gave her another kiss, thrilling everyone. He slipped his arm around her small waist and guided her down the aisle. They smiled for the cameras.

Arm in arm, they strode over to the eastern area designated for the reception. Numerous tables and chairs had been set up as well as tables with a typical buffet of meats, vegetables, and dessert items.

The large mass of people slowly followed behind the happy couple and walked to the reception area for what would be a grand celebration. A long bar was set up in one area of the park, and the people were prepared to party.

Once the orchestra was set up, they played the Baltian national anthem; everyone rose from their seats and sang along with the music. Thomas felt, as the people sung, they were singing to him and his new wife.

"When the orchestra played *The Blue Danube* by Johann Strauss, Thomas took Katie's hand and led her onto the dance floor. This was a favourite waltz of theirs and they floated as if they were two feet above the ground. No one else danced because everybody preferred to watch them.

Thomas and Katie paid little attention to anyone else. As they danced, their eyes were locked on each other's. Their love and strong connection were obvious.

A man dressed in a black jacket and blue jeans stepped in front of the orchestra, and the conductor introduced him as Ed Sheeran. Ed walked to the microphone and sang *How Would You Feel*—a song that held a special meaning for the newlyweds. They danced and swayed to the music.

Suddenly, the couple realized they were alone on the dance floor. With a sweep of his arm, Thomas insisted everyone dance. The people laughed, and couples joined them. Soon the area was covered with dancers.

Thomas whispered in Katie's ear, "Happy?"

Katie lifted her head from his shoulder and gazed into his startling blue eyes. "Oh yes," she whispered back. "So happy."

After dancing for a few more songs, Thomas noticed one of his staff trying to get his attention. He kissed Katie on the forehead, put his arm around her waist, and guided her towards him.

"I'm sorry, sir, but everybody is waiting for you to cut the cake," Ken said, holding a knife.

The couple laughed at their faux pas and glanced at all the people standing around the cake. It was a tall, six-tier, chocolate cake with white icing, with white roses arranged around it. The cake was magnificent, and the couple felt bad cutting into it. They held the knife together and cut two pieces. Thomas fed Katie a piece while she fed him the other piece, and then they kissed. The crowd cheered.

Martin and his wife took over cutting and distributing the cake to the guests.

Thomas whispered in Katie's ear, "Are you hungry?"

"A little. The cake wasn't enough."

The fortunate couple drifted over to the food tables. They each picked up a white china plate with the Baltian crest on it and added some sliced roast beef, steamed broccoli, green beans, and roasted potatoes; a favourite meal for both.

After a few bites, Thomas realized how hungry he was and quickly finished his plate. He hadn't eaten anything since breakfast because he had been so nervous.

Feeling alive again, he leaned towards Katie and said, "I love you."

"I love you, too," Katie replied. She put down her knife and fork and gazed into his eyes. "I will always love you."

"I know." His heart rate increased, and he found himself holding his breath.

Katie smiled. "How long do we have to stay to make it respectable?"

Thomas grinned back, loving her question. "For another few hours. We should allow everyone to congratulate us. Our marriage is bigger than just you and me. We have a role to play."

"Yes," she agreed. "You're right. It's like walking through a portal into a new world. Now, I'm the first lady, and I must set an example."

"You're learning fast," he said. "Let's go and get that work done. Once we get through this, we can leave."

"Is it a secret where we're spending the night?"

"No, it's not in the hotel. I thought you'd prefer to return to the presidential residence. I've had my staff spruce up the place, so I hope you'll feel like it's your home now. You may make any changes you wish."

"Thanks, but there's no rush. I just want to get used to being your wife first."

"You're wonderful." Thomas gave her a long kiss. "Let's soldier ahead and mingle."

When the newlyweds entered the crowd, everyone came up to them to shake their hands and wish them a happy, long life together. The liquor flowed, and everyone got very drunk. Lots of singing and celebrating helped everyone pass the night. No one seemed to get tired of dancing except the newlyweds, who left quietly around two o'clock in the morning.

Chapter Nineteen

While dancing with a pretty blonde woman, Harmon watched the newlyweds leave their celebration. He felt great anger over Thomas's marriage; why should he be so lucky to find a second wife so easily when Harmon hadn't even married once?

It had been many months since Leah's disappearance, and she had still not contacted him. He had heard rumours of where she could be found, but the gossip never led anywhere. He had finally given up ever hearing from her, which was a hard thing to admit. He had shed some tears, but his mourning didn't last too long. He was over her and ready to meet someone new.

Like this attractive blonde woman in his arms. *What was her name again?* The music ended, and Harmon excused himself. He was tired of dancing and all the small chat; he preferred deep discussions about important topics. The women he was meeting couldn't hold a decent conversation, which only angered him.

Harmon was sure about one thing: he didn't want a stupid wife. He required a woman he could show off as well as someone who would elevate his social position. The problem was intelligent women didn't seem interested in him. He had tried to woo a few, but they never worked out because they quickly tired of him.

Out of the corner of his eye, he noticed Silvia Newton standing with some women a few feet away. She had just divorced her second husband over his infidelity. Even though she was a good ten years older than him, he didn't think age mattered. She was known as a flirt, which only inflamed his spirit.

Gathering up his courage, he strode over to the small group. When he stood outside the small circle, he smiled at the ladies, cleared his throat, and said, "Good evening, ladies. How are you all tonight?"

The women glanced at each other, obviously at a loss for what to say. No one said anything for a few moments until Silvia spoke up: "We're very well, thank you. Did you enjoy the wedding?"

"Very much. The first lady looked great." Harmon said what he was expected to say.

"It was such a romantic affair," crooned the woman standing to Silvia's right. Harmon recognized her. She was the wife of the minister of education, but he couldn't remember her name.

The woman to Silvia's left spoke directly to Harmon: "Are you also a romantic?"

"Oh, yes. I'm a very romantic man." Harmon raised his head and noticed Silvia's eyes on him. He turned the question on her.

Silvia giggled. "I might be." She had an infectious laugh, making Harmon smile even though he didn't get the joke.

Harmon coughed and then reached out a hand to her. "Would you care to dance?"

Silvia checked out her friends' expressions. When she finally agreed to his request, Harmon slipped his arm around her shoulders and guided her onto the dance floor.

The music was slow, so he relaxed and led her around the room. He wondered what he must do to seduce her. At the moment, she seemed content.

She interrupted his musings. "Daniel is dancing with Maria."

Harmon noticed the couple. "So what?"

"All they do is criticize each other. I'm surprised they are still together." She kept turning her head to stare at the couple.

"Oh, okay." Harmon was less than interested.

She tapped him on the arm and said, "Oh look. Stephen is talking to Judy."

"So what?" Did he really have to put up with this just to get laid?

"Well, Stephen is a playboy, and Judy is married."

Harmon tried to show some interest, but he really didn't care about those people.

"Look over there," she said as she tightened her hand on his arm.

"Where?" Harmon gazed around the room.

"Over to your left. Margaret is standing alone." She smiled widely.

"So what?" *Not again*. He loosened his grip on her.

"All she talks about is how good it is to be self-sufficient. That's just another way of saying she likes being alone, but she's full of it. She must be lonely."

Harmon moved her to his left just in time to miss another couple. "I really don't care about her."

Silvia gazed seductively at Harmon. She puckered her red lips and feigned a kiss, showing a small dimple on her right cheek. "What do you care about?"

Now they were getting down to business. Harmon stared down at her and whispered, "I'd like to know you better."

A little breathless, Silvia giggled, "You're interested in little ol' me?"

He whispered in her ear, "I think you're a lady who knows how to have fun."

"And what kind of fun is that?" she whispered back.

Harmon smirked. "You know what I mean."

Silvia smiled. "I do."

He brought her hand to his lips and kissed it. "Want to leave?"

She glanced about the room. No one seemed to notice them. "All right. Let's go."

Harmon and Silvia linked fingers. He led her off the dance floor and out the front door. She shivered in the chilly night air. Harmon took off his jacket and placed it around her shoulders.

A valet stood just outside the main doors and, a few moments later, Harmon's car appeared.

As it was brought forward, Silvia said, "Jaguar. Nice."

Harmon's chest puffed out and he breathed a little easier. This night was turning out better than he had expected.

When they were both in the car, Harmon asked, "Do you need anything? We could pick it up on the way."

She leaned back into the seat and replied seductively, "I think you are enough for me."

"You need this as badly as I do, don't you?" He glanced at her out of the corner of his eye. He had to keep his eyes on the road because he was a little drunk and he didn't want to get into an accident.

She sighed loudly. "It's been six months since the divorce and Jim stopped having sex with me at least two years ago."

"Then you are due." He placed a hand on her thigh.

"I'm due." Silvia giggled. "Have you ever dated an older woman?"

"You're not much older," he pointed out as he patted her leg. "But I like a mature woman."

She put her hand on his shoulder and slid it down his arm, reaching his fingers. Her hand left his fingers and moved over to his leg. She trailed her fingers towards his groin and rubbed it.

Harmon was surprised at her forwardness, but he loved it. He pulled over to the side of the road and turned the engine off. After he unzipped his pants, Silvia went down on him.

He couldn't believe his luck. He had been so frustrated. This woman was exactly what he needed. As soon as he was spent, he started up the motor and drove home as quickly as possible.

When they arrived at his house, he jumped out of the car to open her door and together they rushed into the house. He swept her up into his arms and carried her to his bedroom where they had sex all night.

~

The next morning, Harmon had never felt better. A taxi had arrived at seven o'clock to take Silvia home. *What a night*, thought Harmon. He hadn't been that physically active since he was in his twenties. Leah had never stayed the night, even though he often asked her. Silvia pleased him, and he hoped they would continue to meet. He would love something regular with her, but she wouldn't plan another date before she left. "We'll talk," was all she said.

He was in a great mood. He hadn't felt so relieved and relaxed in months. He shook his limbs as he walked to his car, feeling rather free. He had forgotten how much he missed waking up with a woman.

As soon as he turned on the engine, he rolled down the windows. It was a lovely day with blue skies and the sun was shining. A small, refreshing wind blew. He needed to feel the wind clear out the cobwebs from his mind. Today was going to be a good day.

After parking his car in the government parking lot reserved for employees, Harmon walked to the main entrance where a few men stood outside involved in a conversation. Harmon wondered what they were doing there.

They were in his way, which angered Harmon, but, when he approached, they parted to allow him to enter the building. They all bowed their heads and shook his hand.

Once past the group, only one man stood in his way. As he passed by him, Harmon stared into his face and recognized the man immediately. The man stared blankly back. Harmon waited for him to shake his hand, but he didn't.

"Bow to me, you heathen," snarled Harmon.

"Never." Michael turned his back on Harmon and walked away from the building.

Harmon stomped his feet like a child throwing a tantrum.

The group of men turned to look at him. One man asked, "You okay?"

"Fine," Harmon grumbled. He stomped into the building and headed to his office on the third floor.

He was so angry his face had turned a bright shade of red. That man had insulted him for the last time. However, his decree to execute Michael wouldn't take place for a few months. He regretted picking such a late date.

After the cabinet had approved the decree, he had sent the documents to the minister of justice and instructed him to have the gallows built. Once completed, Michael would be hanged for treason. He rubbed his hands and cackled like a witch about to lay a spell.

Chapter Twenty

It had been an active, bustling day, and Thomas was tired. He hadn't slept much last night. He and Katie were getting along better than he ever imagined. Their nights were full of love, but it made the workdays longer.

He picked up the phone and called his secretary. "Would you please come in and bring the President's List?"

The President's List consisted of the names of all the people Thomas had helped over the past year. He liked to have the information brought to him from time to time so he could gauge how his presidency was proceeding.

When the secretary entered his office, Thomas said, "Excuse me, but I'm a little tired. I'm going to lie down on the couch. Would you please read the list?"

"Fine, sir. The first one is Fathi Genadri. You helped him bring his family here from Syria," the secretary read from the papers in her hand.

"Yes, I remember him. How are they doing now?"

"It says he's working as a police officer and his children are attending university."

"Wonderful. What's next?"

"You convinced the government to loan Ben Withers enough money to start his construction company. He's thriving now. He will repay the full sum in the next few months."

"Glad to hear it. I'm going to close my eyes. Please keep reading."

"Fine, sir."

The secretary continued to read aloud the lengthy list, but Thomas dozed off. He woke up with a start, hoping his secretary hadn't noticed. When his ears focussed, he heard her say, "And you owe him a favour."

"Stop there. Read that over." Thomas sat up and threw his legs over the edge of the couch.

"Michael Soros gave you some information that saved your life. You owe him a favour."

"Right. How could I have forgotten?"

"Is there something you'd like to do for him?" asked the secretary, picking up her pen and paper.

"Michael is a hero, but he's a simple man. I don't want to embarrass him, but he does deserve something special." Thomas rose from the couch and paced about the room.

At that moment, there was a loud knock at his office door. The secretary rose from her chair and opened the door. Harmon stood there, carrying a briefcase.

He strode into the room. "I'm ready for the meeting."

"Good." Thomas nodded at his secretary. "We're just in the middle of something. Can you wait?"

"Sure. What's going on?" Harmon put his briefcase on the floor and rested his body against Thomas's desk.

Thomas stopped his pacing and glanced at Harmon. Here was an opportunity to draw Harmon in and see how he responded. "How do you think we should honour a hero?"

Harmon crossed his arms and legs, looking thoughtful. His lips broke into a smile. "There's only one way to honour a hero: he should be paraded around the city."

Thomas was taken aback by his words. A parade? What a great idea, but looking at Harmon, he would bet Harmon was thinking the celebration would be for him. Interesting. Thomas decided to string him along. "Well, now. That's a wonderful idea."

He turned to his secretary. "Would you please arrange a small parade for the hero? He'll be driven around the city."

"Brilliant, sir. It will be arranged. Is that all?"

"Yes. Thank you for your help. Let me know when the parade is arranged."

"Yes, sir." The secretary nodded at her boss. She let herself out of his office and got to work.

Harmon still stood beside Thomas's desk. He seemed happy enough, which made Thomas laugh. Thomas would watch to see how his face would change when Harmon learned Michael was the hero and not him.

Thomas felt wide awake and prepared for his meeting with the Indian president, who was in Baltia to learn how to improve life in India. Thomas had been reviewing Indian society and knew exactly how to better their country.

Thomas glanced at Harmon, noticing he appeared restless. He looked like he had something to say.

Finally, Harmon asked, "Do I know the hero?"

Thomas wasn't ready to reveal the truth. "You may."

"And he'll be paraded around the city?" Harmon stood at attention.

"Yes, he will be, thanks to your suggestion. By the way, did you receive a copy of the Sewell report?"

Harmon appeared preoccupied. "Yes, I did."

"Would you please bring it to me? I want to read it over before it goes to the senate."

"Sure," nodded Harmon. "It's in my office. I'll meet you by the stairs."

Harmon returned to his office to get Thomas the report. Thomas waited a few minutes before heading for the stairwell.

When he reached the stairs, a few of his staff were there discussing the parade. Since it was so nice to have a reason to honour someone, they wanted to make sure the event would be a great success.

When the president approached, one said, "Sir, the day for the parade is Friday, and that day will be announced as a national holiday, so everyone can attend."

"Wonderful."

The staff member standing to his right added, "We have a red convertible for him to ride in."

"Perfect." Thomas was glad he could rely on his staff.

"We've assigned the military band to lead the parade," mentioned another staff member.

"Thanks, everyone," Thomas praised the group. "I appreciate your hard work."

One staff member noticed Harmon approaching them. "Hey, Mr. Sinclair," he called out, "Have you heard the good news?"

"What news?" Harmon asked when he reached the group.

"A parade will be held Friday," announced a staff member. The whole group nodded their heads.

"Yes, I know," said Harmon said with a hint of excitement in his voice.

"We're celebrating a hero," another staff member added.

"I know," replied Harmon. "It's about time that hero is worshipped."

"Do you know the hero?" asked a staff member.

"Do I?" Harmon smiled, expecting the staff to say he was the hero. He put his hands on his hips and stuck out his chest. Then he asked with pride, "So what's the hero's name?"

"Michael," said the staff member. "Michael Soros."

As soon as that man's name was spoken, Harmon blanched. Thomas watched Harmon's face contort. As he realized the parade was being planned for Michael he slouched, and all the light was drawn from his face.

Thomas had kept it a secret that it was Michael who had informed him about the assassins. He hadn't even told his staff. All they knew was Michael had saved the president's life but not any specifics.

However, if Thomas told Harmon what Michael had done, he would really get to see him squirm. Maybe it was time Harmon knew the truth.

Thomas grabbed Harmon by the arm and guided him away from his staff. He moved him against the far wall.

Harmon couldn't break Thomas's strong hold on him. He caught his breath in time to ask: "Why is that man getting the parade?"

Thomas let go of Harmon. With pleasure, he said, "He saved my life."

"How?" Harmon wouldn't look Thomas in the eye.

Thomas whispered, "The assassination."

Harmon backed away from Thomas and seemed to have trouble breathing. He eked out, "What does he have to do with the assassination?"

"He discovered the assassins." Thomas stared straight into Harmon's face and received the answer he wanted. Harmon's face became pale and his jaw dropped.

"How did he learn about them?" Harmon asked. He was visibly shaking.

"He overheard them in the bar." Thomas had to hold himself back from snickering.

Harmon's body quivered. Thomas felt vindicated when he saw how Harmon responded to the news. He was glad to finally get the facts out, and he enjoyed watching Harmon squirm.

But Thomas wasn't prepared to tell him he knew the name of the person who had paid and arranged the assassination. That must be kept a secret for just a little longer.

Chapter Twenty-One

K atie couldn't be happier. As she thought back to her marriage ceremony, she couldn't remember a more romantic time. Thomas had swept her away, making her feel so alive and in love. She wondered if she was dreaming because her life couldn't be better.

Their relationship improved with every moment they spent together. They had developed a perfect understanding, and they could discuss any variety of subjects from children to card games to pets. The more they talked, the more they realized how much they had in common. Communication was the key, and neither had any trouble expressing themselves.

Though they spent their wedding night in the presidential residence, Thomas had planned a special trip to a small, private spot in the Cayman Islands. There they were treated like royalty with a private beach house on the water. They spent their days walking the beach and swimming in the ocean.

When it was time to return home, they were ready to face the world as the presidential couple. Thomas had coached Katie in her special duties as first lady. He had explained how to behave at different functions and events when her presence would be required. She was prepared to accept her new position.

While Thomas was busy running the country, Katie found a few charities in which to get involved. One concerned the building of the children's mental health centre, and she involved her friend, Andrea. Between them, they worked out ways to bring the centre to life.

Though the centre kept her busy, Katie found time to visit several hospitals. Most of her time was spent in the children's ward where she gave each child warm words of encouragement. She showed the parents kindness and respect as they stayed strong for their children. With her smile and kind words, Katie spread happiness and optimism.

And Katie had a secret: she thought she was pregnant. It had been a month since the wedding, and she should have had her period by now. She didn't want to tell Thomas until she was completely sure and she'd had an appointment with the doctor. Thomas would be ecstatic with this news.

Tonight, Thomas had a late meeting so she invited Michael to join her for dinner. They had kept in contact, but they hadn't seen each other since the wedding. She was excited to show him around and to tell him about her wonderful life.

Just before five o'clock, Michael arrived out of breath. The butler showed him to Katie's favourite sitting room, and he ran into the room looking dishevelled and upset. His uncombed brown hair fell about his face. Katie had never seen her cousin in such a frazzled state.

When they were alone, Katie asked, "Michael, what's the matter?" She showed him to the couch, then walked over to a table and poured him a glass of water.

"Thank you," Michael muttered as she handed him the glass.

She perched beside him on the couch. "What happened?"

Michael took a long drink of the water before he could speak. "There's a decree to have me executed."

Katie was shocked. "What decree?"

"On March thirteenth, I will be hanged."

"What?" Katie couldn't believe her ears.

"The cabinet passed a decree to have me executed. They think I planned the assassination."

"Executed? You?" Katie felt out of breath. She felt Michael's arm around her and she settled down.

"Yes," Michael whispered.

She shook her head. "What are we going to do?"

Katie peered into Michael's face looking for inspiration. A few moments later, she said, "I'll go to Thomas to ask him to annul the decree."

Michael grabbed her hand. "Yes, of course."

"But I don't understand why he'd agree to such a decree. He knows you're my cousin." Katie tried to make sense of this.

Michael inhaled deeply and then let the air out slowly. "Maybe this is why you became the first lady. You were meant to save me."

While Katie's eyes locked on Michael's, there was a knock on the door. A maid entered the room.

Standing on the threshold, she said, "Madam, dinner is ready."

Katie glanced over at Michael, and he nodded his head. They followed the maid into the dining room where a delicious meal of roast chicken with scalloped potatoes and steamed asparagus had been prepared for them. Once their glasses were full of white wine and their plates were before them, the maids left them alone.

Not much discussion arose from the two during the meal, and Katie only picked at her food. She knew what she must do, but she worried about the decree. Why would Thomas agree to such a thing, and who had written it?

Michael seemed able to read her thoughts because he said, "I don't know who wrote it."

"I'll find out," Katie said. She put down her fork and knife on the plate and stared down at her food. The wheels were spinning in her head. She needed courage and strength to determine what was going on here.

"I'm so proud of you. You'll save my life." Michael had been watching her face scrunch up and then smile.

Just then, the maids came in to clear the table. One maid brought out cups of coffee. In silence, Michael and Katie picked up their cups and walked out of the dining room. They returned to Katie's sitting room where they had more privacy.

Katie sipped at her coffee. It was hot and she could feel the caffeine surge through her body. She felt clear-headed. "Who would want you dead?"

Michael shook his head. "No idea."

"Think," said Katie. "Have you had an argument with anyone?"

"Not at the butcher shop. Wait," he hesitated.

"What?" She placed a hand on his arm.

"I refused to bow to the vice-president and shake his hand, but I can't imagine that's reason enough to have me executed." Michael brought a finger up to his chin and rubbed his stubble.

"He's a vicious man. I don't trust him," admitted Katie. "I wouldn't put it past him to be so malicious."

Michael placed his hands over his face and bowed his head. "He was so mad at me his face turned red. I thought his head was going to explode."

She shook her head. "Then why didn't you bow to him?"

"Bow to him? He's a horrible man. Did you know he's the one who hired the assassins?" Michael caught his breath. He should not have said that.

"Harmon hired the men to assassinate Thomas?" She was shocked. "How do you know that?"

Michael sighed and took a few moments to reply. "I overheard the assassins in the pub. I warned the president, which is why the assassins failed. He swore me to secrecy."

"Don't worry," she said while patting his hand. "He won't know I possess this knowledge. I'll prepare a special dinner for Thomas and invite Harmon. I will bring up the decree and see how they respond."

"You must tread carefully," said Michael. "Harmon is a dangerous man."

"I know, but he'll never know my true intention. Thomas will annul the decree."

"Thank you, my dear. You're a strong woman and my champion."

Katie ran into his open arms, and they hugged tightly. She drew as much strength from him as she could. Michael placed his hands on either side of her face and kissed her on the forehead. Katie thanked him with a wide smile. One small tear escaped her eye.

Chapter Twenty-Two

As had become habit, Katie waited by the front door for Thomas to return home from work. This was a tradition she began on his first day back to work as a married man. He kept his days pretty regular, so he would punctually return by half past seven. She loved that about him.

Even though she kept herself busy during the day, she always missed Thomas. He brought such light into her life. When they were apart, she felt like something was missing. When they were together, she felt complete.

She found marriage easier than she had thought. In her teens, she had a few boyfriends, but none close to marriage. She always had men interested in her, but she didn't fall in love with any of them.

Love was very important to her, and she had found true love with Thomas. She was determined to do anything she could to make his life better. Since he enjoyed seeing her as soon as he returned from work, she waited every day with a ready martini and a kiss.

Her parents had been the perfect role models, and she could only hope for such a marriage. She wished they could have seen her happily married to such a wonderful man. She was sure they would approve of him and accept him into their family.

However, she hadn't expected to fall in love as hard as she had. Thomas was everything any woman would want, but chemistry was something she couldn't predict. Both were amazed how well they got along.

Katie heard crunching gravel, proving a car was in the driveway. She then heard a door slam shut. She smiled as she heard his footsteps clunk on the paved walkway that soon reached the front door. His confident strides brought butterflies to Katie's stomach.

When he passed over the threshold, Katie slid off the bench and walked towards him. She gave Thomas a beaming smile. "Welcome home, sweetheart." She reached up to kiss him, and then she handed him a martini.

"Thank you, my love," said Thomas. "This is perfect."

He gratefully accepted the glass and had a good, long sip. Then he encircled her waist with his arms and brought her towards him, giving her a passionate kiss.

For a few moments, the couple stood there leaning against each other and giving each other soft kisses. Their bodies moulded well, and their passion was obvious to anyone who saw them together.

Katie always marvelled at how well her husband smelled. Every morning, she saw him shave and then put some cologne on his face, but she couldn't smell it unless she was close to him. And she loved being that close. She felt lost in his scent.

"Would you like dinner now? Or eat later?" she asked after he had finished off the drink.

Playing with the empty glass, he replied, "I'm not in any rush to eat. Would you like to join me upstairs?"

Katie laughed. He was always so direct. She placed her hand in his and guided him towards the staircase. They climbed the steps holding hands. When they reached the landing, they stared into each other eyes. He picked her up, carried her into their bedroom, and gently placed her on the bed.

As she looked into his eyes, she only saw love and happiness. He was gentle yet confident when holding her, and she enjoyed learning how to please him. Their lovemaking was just that: an expression of their love.

Afterwards, they lay in each other's arms, catching their breath. Neither moved because neither wished to break the amazing spell. But tonight, Katie had something to tell him.

She raised herself up on one elbow and looked down into the dark blue eyes she had come to love. She was so excited she could hardly contain herself. This was the news she was thrilled to share because she knew how much it meant to him.

Once she was sitting upright, she said, "I have a present for you."

Thomas rolled towards her. "Your love is enough of a gift. As far as I'm concerned, everything else is a bonus."

"Well, I have that bonus." Katie enjoyed seeing the look of happy expectation on his face.

She opened the cabinet beside the bed and pulled out a small red box. She held it in her hands a moment, breathed deeply, and then held the box out to him.

Thomas bolted upright with his back against the bed frame. He took the box from his wife and opened it. Inside was a pacifier. His eyes opened wide and his jaw fell. He tipped the box towards his wife and asked, "Does this mean what I think it means?"

"Yes." A huge smile covered her face.

Thomas stopped breathing and then whispered, "You're pregnant?"

Katie nodded.

He threw his arms around her and kissed her. "You've made me the happiest man alive. I love you."

Katie laughed as he continued to kiss her all over her body. He spent some time nuzzling her stomach where his child was growing. They made love again.

Thomas trailed a finger around her face, which Katie found very sensual. He then brushed her hair back and tickled her neck. He kissed her as she laughed.

With his lips near her ears, he whispered, "I don't want to get dressed, but I'm hungry."

She kissed his fingers, then his lips, and said, "Why don't we have dinner in bed?"

"What would you like?"

"Anything would be great."

Thomas picked up the phone and called the kitchen. He arranged to have dinner brought up but left outside the door. The staff did as ordered.

"I have some good news for you," Thomas said after he had finished eating. He picked up her hands and held them tight.

She brought his hand up to her lips and whispered, "And what would that be?"

He held her hands still and put on a serious face. "Let me ask you this: Did your cousin Michael ever tell you what he did for me?"

Katie knew this topic would come up at some point. Thomas was aware of how close she was with Michael. She stared into his blue eyes and said, "He told me about the assassins."

Thomas breathed a little easier. As he exhaled, he said, "Did he tell you everything?"

"Yes, he did." Katie wasn't quite ready to reveal any more of their discussion because this was not the time. Under no condition would she bring up the decree.

Thomas put his hand under her chin, raised her mouth to his, and kissed her. "We're holding a parade for him tomorrow. He'll be driven down the main street and honoured."

Katie clapped her hands. "That's wonderful."

"I owe him so much, and he never asked for any reward. That's why the parade will be perfect."

"Yes, I agree. Michael is a wonderful man. I love him like a father."

Thomas threw off the sheet and slid his legs over the edge of the bed. He stood up and stretched his arms over his head. He turned around and said, "Is he content to be the butcher?"

Katie laughed. "That's a funny question. He's never complained about it."

"Do you think he would be interested in a government job?"

"I have no idea. Why don't you ask him?"

Thomas considered her words. "I think I will."

"What position would be appropriate for him?"

"Not sure. I'll have to think about that, but I'll ask him first if he'd be willing to leave his butcher shop."

"What time is the parade?" asked Katie.

"At ten o'clock in the morning. A stage has been set up for us to sit on. I'll have the car bring you to the podium where I'll be waiting. Now come here."

Thomas lay down on the bed, and Katie wiggled over to him. He reached out and enveloped her in his arms. Their passionate kisses inspired their lovemaking. It was tender and sweet. Afterwards, they fell asleep in each other's arms.

Chapter Twenty-Three

As expected, the hero's parade was a grand success. Michael was driven down Graton's main street in a bright red convertible. He lounged on the flat trunk with both feet resting on the back seat, a huge smile shining on his happy face. With both hands, he waved to the people who had come out to cheer and clap as he passed.

Katie was so proud of him. He deserved to be honoured and this parade was a great idea. She stood with her husband and several important people on a platform midway down the street. They all waved as Michael cruised by.

Only one important person was absent from the parade, and Katie wondered if her husband had noticed the vice-president was not present. She didn't think he would be missed, but she thought it quite apropos. Harmon's absence proved to her that everything Michael had told her was true.

After all the shaking of hands, Thomas reached over to Katie and whispered in her ear, "We can get out of here now. Why don't we go home and have a nap before I have to get back to the office?"

Katie was pleased with his suggestion. She grabbed his left arm and held on tight as he guided her away from the crowd.

As soon as they were settled in the limousine, Thomas leaned over and said, "I'm sorry, but I should have said earlier how pretty you look today. How are you feeling, my pregnant wife?"

"Just great," Katie said. She planted a kiss on his lips. "I love being pregnant. I feel so amazing knowing our child is growing inside of me."

Thomas reached out and rubbed Katie's stomach. He let his hand linger there for a few moments. "Having any problems?"

"Just a little morning sickness, but that's normal. The doctor said I shouldn't have any problems. I'm healthy."

"You sure look healthy to me." Thomas smiled and then kissed her. "Let's discuss names."

Katie laughed. "Isn't it a bit early for that? I'm just hoping the baby is healthy."

"It's never too early. Do you have any favourites?"

"I've always loved Sarah for a girl and Alexander for a boy." Katie placed a hand on his cheek and ran her hand down his jaw line.

"They are both good names. I like Rebecca for a girl and Peter for a boy. We can incorporate both our choices."

"Those are good, too, but I think we need to see the child first before we decide on a name."

Thomas kissed her again. "Fine. We'll wait."

After the limousine pulled into their driveway, the couple dashed into the house and up to their bedroom. Before entering, Thomas swept her up into his arms and carried her to the bed. Their lovemaking was passionate.

After they were spent and lying in each other's arms, Thomas asked, "Would you like to go shopping for the baby?"

"Then everyone will know I'm pregnant. I'd like to keep it a secret for a little while longer." Katie wasn't sure she was ready to announce her pregnancy to the world.

"I understand. We can go whenever you want. Or would you like the staff to get us everything?"

"No, I think it would be fun to go shopping with you and pick out what we need like any parents who are expecting. Let's just wait a couple of months until my pregnancy is obvious, okay?"

"Sure," Thomas agreed. He picked up her discarded dress and laid it on the end of the bed. "Your floral dress sure looked wonderful on you. I much prefer your simple sense of fashion to Leah's over-the-top wardrobe. The amount of money she spent on clothes never ceased to amaze me."

"Your marriage sounded terrible. Why did you marry her?" This was a question Katie had been dying to ask him since they started dating. She was glad the subject had finally come up.

"I was young and stupid," Thomas replied.

"Have you matured?"

"Oh, my love, you've changed my feelings towards marriage. When Leah left, I considered never marrying again, but I wanted children. I worried how I would choose the next Mrs. Edmonds."

"I can understand that. Being the president, you must be wary of the false. I hope you know I would never lie to you. I prefer being completely honest. Then there's less to remember." Katie laughed.

"I know, my dear, and I'll always be honest with you. I want no more games. You please me more than you can ever know." Thomas wound his arms about her shoulders and hugged her tight.

Katie felt so secure and loved being in his arms, but her body stiffened.

Thomas asked, "What's the matter?"

She remained still and silent for a few moments. She looked up into his eyes, and said, "Do you love me?"

"Of course I do," he answered immediately.

"Would you allow me to invite Harmon over for dinner tonight?"

Thomas looked truly astounded. "Why would you want that man in our house?"

She placed a hand on his arm. "I have something to reveal to him, and I need to see his response."

Thomas gave her a generous kiss on the lips. "I'm sorry for acting this way, but the man is a traitor. That fact will be revealed to the country soon."

"Until you do, could you please do me this favour?"

"Okay, I will. I'll bring Harmon home with me."

They held each other for a few minutes as Thomas planted little kisses on her lips. Katie loved this attention.

Thomas looked at the clock. It was time for him to return to work. He kissed Katie once more and then said, "I've got to go. See you tonight. I hope you know what you're doing."

"Don't worry. All will be revealed tonight."

"Okay, my love, I'll comply with your wishes. See you tonight." Thomas jumped out of bed, took a shower, and when dressed, he blew a goodbye kiss to Katie and left her alone in the bedroom.

Katie promptly tucked herself in for a nap. She felt tired much more often now she was pregnant. A good afternoon nap was exactly what she needed, and rest was necessary before confronting Harmon.

Chapter Twenty-Four

Harmon was angry. His meeting with the Russian delegation didn't go as planned. They wouldn't discuss anything with him. They demanded to speak only with the president. Harmon wanted to shout, "Don't you know who I am?"

After leaving the Russians, he withdrew into his office and slammed his door. He immediately walked over to his liquor cabinet, pulled out a bottle of scotch, and poured himself a generous portion. Once he had a few sips, he flopped onto the couch. He moved his legs onto the pillows and relaxed. He wouldn't let those men get to him. Once he was president, he would show them who's boss.

After he had finished a glass, he stumbled over to his desk to check his emails. There were several he had to deal with. He checked his notes and replied to the people asking for a meeting or those confirming appointments.

Just as he finished writing his last email, he received a new one. A little distracted, he opened it and read it quickly, then read it over again because he couldn't believe his eyes: Katie had invited him over for dinner. He was surprised by the request. He accepted her invitation out of curiosity.

She wrote back: "Glad to hear it. You can drive over with Thomas. He'll meet you after work."

Harmon ruminated over the invitation. He couldn't help but wonder why he was being invited over to their house. He poured himself another glass of scotch and sipped it slowly, letting the liquor roll around in his mouth.

He was still confident Thomas knew nothing about his involvement with the assassins. If he knew, he would have accused him of treason by now. Harmon felt sure his treason would never see the light of day. He was surprised the assassins had remained so loyal to him, but it had saved him.

Glancing at his watch, he realized the hour was getting late and Thomas would show up soon. He moved into the bathroom and washed his face with soap and water, combed his thin black hair, and adjusted his tie. He didn't want to look like he had been drinking.

He walked over to his desk and plopped down onto his reclining leather chair, but he didn't feel like working. He waited for the inevitable knock on the door.

He didn't have to wait too long. When he heard the knock, Harmon rose from his chair, walked over to the door, and opened it.

Thomas stood there. "Finished with your day?"

"All done here," replied Harmon.

"Ready to go?"

"Ready."

They didn't talk as they made their way down to the president's limousine. Both were concentrating on their own thoughts. Harmon could only guess what Thomas was thinking. Did Katie tell him the reason for the invitation?

Once inside the car, Thomas picked a bottle of rye and held it up for Harmon. "Want a drink for the road?"

"Sounds good." Harmon accepted the glass from Thomas.

Once they had finished their first glass, Harmon's tongue loosened and he asked, "Why was I invited over tonight?"

"I have no idea," said Thomas. "This was all Katie's idea. Would you like another?"

Harmon nodded his head. Even though he felt a little drunk, he wouldn't refuse the alcohol.

Katie was in the kitchen when Thomas and Harmon arrived for dinner. The butler ushered them into the dining room, and they sat down at the table. Katie came out of the kitchen and welcomed them. She was dressed in a pretty, pale pink dress with her hair flowing down her back. Both men rose from their chairs.

Katie strolled over to her husband and asked, "How was your day, dear?"

"Busy, but good." He leaned over and kissed her.

She nodded to Harmon while she made her way to the other end of the table to take her seat. As she lowered herself onto her chair, the men joined her and sat down.

"Thank you for the invitation," Harmon said as he adjusted his chair.

"My pleasure," Katie replied, as she shot him a brilliant smile. "So glad you were available."

"I'd have changed any plans to have dinner with the president and the first lady," Harmon gushed. His effusiveness caused Katie's skin to crawl and Thomas's stomach to turn.

Katie took a breath. "Would you care for some wine?"

At that moment, a waiter entered the dining room carrying a bottle of red wine. He filled their glasses and then left the bottle on the table beside Thomas.

"What should we drink to?" Thomas asked, picking up his glass.

Katie held up her glass. "Let's drink to family."

"Strange toast," muttered Harmon.

Thomas raised his glass. "To family."

They touched glasses in the air and then sipped their wine.

The kitchen door opened and two waiters approached the table with plates filled with various kinds of meat, potatoes, and salad. They placed them on the table before silently leaving the dining room.

"And what do we have here?" Thomas said as he looked over the dishes.

"An assortment of meats from a local butcher's shop. I thought we could try them," Katie said as she sat back to watch the men try the food.

Thomas served himself a slice of roast beef, a piece of sausage, and a pork chop. He added some mashed potatoes and salad onto his dinner plate. Harmon did the same.

"Not bad," said Thomas. "This is a nice dinner. I'm really enjoying the meats. What do you think, Harmon?"

"Good," mumbled Harmon with a full mouth.

Thomas glanced over at his wife and asked, "So which butcher do we have to thank for this delicious meal?"

"Michael Soros," Katie replied.

Harmon choked. He brought up his napkin to his mouth and coughed a few times, then reached for his water glass and swallowed half its contents. He coughed a few more times before wiping his mouth with his napkin.

When he was finally able to speak, he said, "This is from Soros's butcher shop?"

"Yes," Katie said, a slight smile playing on her lips. "Do you like it?"

"Well, I sure do," answered Thomas. "There are some good flavours here." He peered into Harmon's face and asked, "What do you think?"

"This is from Michael Soros?" was all Harmon could utter. He spit the food in his mouth into his napkin. "What are you trying to do here?"

"What do you mean?" Katie asked as innocently as possible.

"Don't you know about the decree?" spat Harmon. He pushed his plate into the centre of the table.

"What decree?" Katie enquired.

Katie noticed Thomas looked confused. She wasn't sure he understood. Now, it was Katie's turn to be surprised.

It was Harmon who explained. "The decree to execute Michael Soros for treason."

"I signed that decree?" Thomas's eyes widened and he raised his eyebrows.

"Yes, you did. We met in your office a couple of months ago. We discussed the decree, and you agreed to sign it," Harmon enunciated his words making sure Thomas understood.

Thomas shook his head. "I don't remember that. Can I see this decree?"

Harmon called over a servant and insisted he bring his briefcase to him. Thomas and Katie waited in silence.

After a few moments, the man returned with Harmon's briefcase. As soon as it was in his hands,

Harmon opened it, rifled through some papers, and withdrew a folder. Harmon handed the paper inside the folder to Thomas.

"That's not my signature." Thomas said, looking at the decree.

"Of course it is," interjected Harmon. "You were a little drunk when you signed it."

Thomas shook his head and coughed. "I don't remember signing this." He read aloud, "On March thirteenth, Michael Soros will be executed for treason."

He stared at Harmon who placed his arms on the table as if daring him to dispute the decree.

"Why did you create such a decree?" Katie asked.

Harmon puffed out his chest. "Michael Soros is rude and disobedient. He was the one who planned and paid for your assassination."

"I don't believe that." Katie shook her head.

Thomas sneered, "Can you prove it?"

Thomas and Katie stopped eating to wait for Harmon's response. They watched his expression.

Harmon, undeterred, said, "I have proof."

"What is it?" Thomas asked while holding his knife aloft. He appeared a little menacing.

"Well, Michael was at the bar at the same time as the assassins," Harmon reminded him. He straightened his back to sit as erect as possible. He intended to show strength, but he didn't know both Thomas and Katie knew he was lying.

"Do you have any evidence to show Michael talked to the assassins?" Thomas had every intention of putting Harmon down now.

"It's in my files," Harmon said, attempting to sidetrack the discussion.

"I want to see that," said Thomas.

Harmon moved his plate, picked up his briefcase, and placed it on the dining room table.

"You wrote this decree to get revenge on one man?" asked Katie in horror.

Harmon snarled, "If one misbehaves, then the rest will surely follow."

"But what if they don't? Is that reason enough to have him executed?" Katie demanded.

She brushed down the front of her dress and then folded her hands together in front of her. She glared at Harmon. "Michael Soros is my cousin, and he has been like a father to me since my parents died."

Harmon jumped from his chair. He glanced at Thomas who was sitting perfectly still, watching his every move.

"You're his cousin?" asked Harmon. His eyes bulged and his jaw hung open.

"Yes," Katie said as she took Thomas's hand in hers.

"I take great offence to this meal," Harmon fumed. His face turned red and his fists were clenched. He scraped his chair loudly on the floor as he pushed it back. He stood up with his hands on his hips and stuck out his chest.

Suddenly, Thomas rose from his chair and walked out of the room. Katie's eyes followed her husband's movements. Harmon seemed shocked by Thomas's departure.

Harmon turned to Katie and asked, "What are you doing?"

Katie looked up at him. "What do you mean?"

For a short moment, he took his eyes off her to pour himself another glass of wine. He sipped it and then said, "Why are you getting involved in this?"

Katie shrugged her shoulders. "I'm not going to allow you to execute my cousin just because you don't like him."

Harmon scoffed. "Your relationship will make no difference."

"How can you say that? You want to murder *my cousin*."

Harmon stood in front of her chair. He leaned over and put his hands on her shoulders. He was about to speak when Thomas walked back into the room.

Thomas bellowed, "Get your hands off her!"

Harmon jumped away from Katie. "I'm not doing anything."

"I know what I saw. Guards!" Thomas called out.

Two beefy men in uniform entered the dining room and halted in front of Thomas.

"Arrest that man," said Thomas, pointing to Harmon.

The bodyguards marched up to Harmon and grabbed his arms. They kept looking from Thomas to Harmon, waiting for the charge.

As Harmon's body shook, he shouted, "Arrest me? Why? I wasn't doing anything."

Thomas snorted. "I know what I saw."

"I wasn't doing anything," Harmon shouted. "It's ridiculous for you to arrest me for nothing."

"How about I arrest you for the crime of treason?" Thomas asked, looking straight at Harmon.

Harmon's eyes opened wide. "What are you talking about?"

"I know you planned the assassination," stated Thomas.

Harmon fainted. The guards picked him up and carried him out of the room. They put him in a car and drove him to the prison where he was put into a cell with nothing more than a bed, sink, and toilet.

He was thrown onto a simple, hard bed where he buried his head in his hands and cried. He cried for his predicament, and he cried for his loss. He would never be president now, and he had lost his freedom. He had lost everything, and now he would lose his life, too: the only penalty for treason was death by hanging.

But he had one chance. There would be a trial and he could hire his own lawyer. There was only one for him; if anyone could get him off, this man could. Harmon looked forward to having his say in court. Anything could happen.

Chapter Twenty-Five

Shown into the prison meeting room, Harmon sat down in one of the two metal chairs. He placed his arms on the cold metal table and waited for his lawyer to arrive. Harmon had hired Albert Moss, the best (and most expensive) defence trial lawyer in Baltia, and he was late.

Suddenly, the door creaked open and his lawyer stood on the threshold. He looked dapper in his grey suit, cream shirt, and a green tie. His grey hair was cut short, and based on the way he combed it, it was obvious he was trying to hide some balding. Albert Moss sauntered over to the other metal chair and sat down. He placed his briefcase on the table and opened it.

Mr. Moss pulled out a pack of cigarettes and an ashtray. He handed Harmon a lighter and said, "I heard you smoke."

"Yes, thanks," replied Harmon. He ripped open the pack of cigarettes, extracted one, and lit it with the red, plastic lighter. He inhaled deeply and then exhaled slowly, allowing the smoke to flow around his lungs. After a few more puffs, he felt better.

"First," said Mr. Moss. "I need you to sign this contract confirming you have hired me to represent you at the trial."

He slid the paper across the table and pulled a pen out from his breast jacket pocket. He handed the pen to Harmon who read the contract. There was nothing in it causing Harmon any concern. It was a typical contract, and he had signed many of them.

Once Harmon signed, the lawyer signed and dated it in the appropriate places. He then took out a stamp and placed it on the contract, notarizing it.

Mr. Moss shuffled some papers in his briefcase and brought out a yellow legal pad. When he was prepared, he glanced at Harmon. "Tell me everything."

Harmon told him the whole story. He didn't know how much Thomas was aware of, so he had to apprise his lawyer of the complete situation. He spoke for at least ten minutes before he was finished.

"So you had an affair with the president's wife and hired men to assassinate him?" Mr. Moss summed up Harmon's words.

"Yes. I guess it sounds pretty bad for me." Harmon laughed nervously.

"And until the president accused you of treason, he has never given you any indication he is aware of these facts?"

"Right. Leah might have said something to him. She was pretty mad at him for the breakup, but I'm not sure." Harmon lit another cigarette. It sure felt good to smoke.

Mr. Moss made a few notes. "Where can I find Leah?"

Tapping his cigarette on the ashtray, Harmon replied, "No idea. She's disappeared."

"Okay. We probably won't need her," said Mr. Moss. He flipped the page. "Could anyone tie you to the assassins?"

"I was in a public bar. Anyone could have seen us."

"Then we'll have to assume someone has come forward." Mr. Moss scribbled words onto the page. "Do you have anything material to tie you to the assassins?"

Harmon thought back. He had destroyed all their emails, but they could be recovered by a computer specialist. "No, I don't think so."

Mr. Moss nodded his head.

"Wait," said Harmon. He stubbed out his cigarette. "I did give them a handwritten list of the president's daily routine."

"Well, that's something. We'll have to assume the prosecutor has that." Mr. Moss turned to another fresh page and continued to make notes.

"Doesn't look good for me, does it?"

"No," Mr. Moss admitted, shaking his head. "It doesn't, but you deserve a defence, and I'll give you a good one."

Mr. Moss stood up and stuck out his hand. Harmon grabbed it and they shook, giving Harmon a little confidence.

"I'm going now," Mr. Moss said as he threw his legal pad and pen into his briefcase. "I'll keep you apprised of the situation. The trial takes place Monday morning at nine. Do you have any fresh clothes to wear?"

Looking down at his rumpled suit, Harmon answered, "No. I just have this."

"I'll have someone go to your home and pick up something for you to wear. Anything you need? Anything I can get for you?"

Harmon shook his head. "No."

There was nothing he wanted. There was nothing he needed. He had lost everything. Everything was gone.

Chapter Twenty-Six

The courtroom was packed for Harmon's trial. When Harmon strode out the side door and into the courtroom, with his lawyer by his side, he felt only animosity from the crowd. He had no friends here, and he was sure what friends he had would desert him now.

After Mr. Moss took his place at the head of the table, Harmon lowered himself into the wooden chair beside him. He kept his eyes on the table, afraid to look around. In his peripheral vision, he noticed the prosecutor. Even though Harmon had little to do with him, he considered the prosecutor a decent fellow who was devoted to the law. They had met several times in the past at social events, but they had not said more than a few words to each other.

There was no jury at a treason trial. The court couldn't trust a jury to remain unbiased because treason was such a serious crime. The trial would be decided by only a judge and, for this trial, Judge Russell Martin presided. He was an older man and a long tenant of the law. He had announced at the trial's press conference he was retiring. This trial would be his last.

A young man in a guard's uniform standing by the witness box shouted, "Everyone please rise for Judge Martin."

Everyone in the courtroom stood up.

Judge Martin, dressed in a black robe with a white collar, marched into the courtroom and stepped up to his seat behind a huge wooden podium. After he was settled, the rest of the room returned to their chairs, making a lot of scrapping noises.

A court attendant passed a piece of paper to the young guard. Reading aloud, the guard said, "This is case 473 in the matter of the Country of Baltia versus Harmon Sinclair. The charge is treason."

A hush came over the room.

The judge shuffled a few papers, and then said, "Okay, Mr. Pearce, you may begin."

The prosecutor stood up. "We are here because the defendant, Harmon Sinclair, has committed treason against Baltia. We have proof the defendant hired two foreign men to assassinate our president."

Harmon slumped in his chair. *They knew.* Harmon wasn't that surprised, but he wanted to face his informer. He thought back to his meeting with the assassins and tried to remember who was around them, but he hadn't paid much attention to the bar's occupants. He berated himself for not paying more attention.

The judge nodded his head. "What says the defendant?"

Harmon's lawyer stood. "Not guilty."

The judge turned to the prosecutor. "Mr. Pearce, please call your first witness."

"Our first witness is," said Mr. Pearce, pausing for effect, "Michael Soros."

Harmon's jaw dropped to the floor. Could he ever be free of that man?

The guard said, "Come forward, Michael Soros."

Harmon heard Michael's heavy footsteps on the hardwood floor before he saw him. It was a very irritating sound.

Michael walked straight past the lawyers and Harmon and up to the witness box. Once he was settled in the wooden chair, Mr. Pearce moved to stand before him.

"Please state your name and occupation."

Michael folded his hands in his lap, looked up at the judge, and said, "My name is Michael Soros. I'm the butcher."

Mr. Pearce waited until Michael looked his way before continuing. "Where were you on the night of Friday, November third, one year ago?"

"I was having a few beers with some friends at Le Lion."

Mr. Pearce put a hand on the back of Michael's chair and asked, "That's the bar out on the main highway?"

"Yes," Michael confirmed.

Mr. Pearce sauntered over to his table, picked up a piece of paper, looked at it, and then said, "Would you please relate the events of the night on Friday, November third at Le Lion?"

Michael cleared his throat. "I noticed two scruffy men at a booth drinking a lot of beer."

Mr. Pearce nodded his head. "Did you know either of these men?"

"No."

"What happened next?" the prosecutor asked, looking at the paper in his hand.

Michael glared at Harmon. "I saw Mr. Sinclair join those men."

Harmon was shocked by Michael's intense stare. The man was out to get him. He didn't remember seeing Michael at the bar, but he had obviously been close enough to the booth to identify the assassins. It angered him to no end he had misjudged the situation.

"You mean the defendant?" asked Mr. Pearce, pointing at Harmon.

Michael nodded his head. "Yes."

Mr. Pearce moved in front of the judge's desk. "Go on."

"They were together for maybe half an hour," Michael said, glancing at his wrist watch.

Mr. Pearce held up his hand and asked, "Did you overhear their conversation?"

Michael nodded again. "There was a lot of noise in the bar, but I could hear a few words."

"What did you hear them say?" pressed the prosecutor.

Michael crossed his legs. "Mr. Sinclair hired them to kill the president."

It sounded as if the entire audience inhaled their breath at the same moment. Harmon felt every eye on the back of his head.

Mr. Pearce pushed, "Are you sure?"

"Yes, very. I saw Mr. Sinclair hand them a thick, white envelope."

"Do you know what was in that envelope?"

Mr. Moss stood up and objected, "Circumstantial evidence, Your Honour. Unless Mr. Soros saw what was inside the envelope, he can have no idea what was in it."

"Question withdrawn," conceded Mr. Pearce.

He walked over to the table, picked up another piece of paper, and read it quickly before putting it down. He turned to Michael. "What did you do with this information?"

Michael uncrossed his legs. "I met with the president at his office during his public audience."

"And you revealed all you had heard?" asked Mr. Pearce.

"Yes," replied Michael.

166

"Thank you, Mr. Soros. No more questions," said Mr. Peace.

The judge turned to Mr. Moss. "You may now question the witness."

Harmon's lawyer rose slowly from his chair and walked around to the witness box. Once he stood in front of Michael, he asked, "You were in a busy, noisy bar, is that correct?"

Michael answered, "Yes, that's true but..."

Mr. Moss interrupted him. "So you couldn't clearly overhear what my client said to those men?"

"I could hear well enough." Michael was perched on the edge of his seat.

"Over that noisy crowd?" Mr. Moss laughed as if what Michael said were incredible.

"Yes, I did," Michael replied indignantly. He placed his feet flat on the floor and straightened his back.

"Your Honour, I stipulate this man couldn't be sure of the words spoken by my client."

"The court will take that into consideration," said the judge. "Do you have any further questions?"

"Yes, Your Honour."

"Then proceed," directed the judge.

"Mr. Soros, was it true you were drinking beer that night?" Mr. Moss asked, while staring at a piece of paper in his hand.

"Yes, but ..." said Michael.

Again Mr. Moss interrupted him. "Do you remember how many beers you had?"

Michael's eyes looked left as he tried to remember the number. He murmured, "Two or three?"

"Are you sure?"

"Yes, sir."

"How would you like to know you had five beers that night?" accused Mr. Moss.

"I don't remember." Michael looked at his feet.

"So you could have possibly been too drunk to overhear any conversation in the bar that night?" Mr. Moss asked.

Michael raised his eyes and said to the judge, "I wasn't drunk."

"Your honour, I again stipulate this man was too drunk to be sure of any conversation held in the bar that night," Mr. Moss charged.

The judge said, "I will take that into consideration. Please go on."

"Mr. Soros, is it true you have an issue with my client?"

Harmon smiled. He had told his lawyer all about Michael's insolence and impertinence.

Michael looked confused. "I don't know what you mean."

Mr. Moss put his hands on his hips and accused, "You refused to pay the vice-president proper respect."

Michael smirked. "I have no respect for a traitor."

Mr. Moss looked at Harmon and then back at Michael. "Was that your reason?"

"Yes," Michael stately clearly.

"No more questions, Your Honour." Mr. Moss returned to his chair.

Harmon tapped Mr. Moss on the shoulder, but he shook his head to indicate not to disturb him. Harmon felt uncomfortable with Michael's testimony.

"You may leave the witness stand," the judge directed Michael.

With a big smile aimed at Harmon, Michael returned to his seat in the audience.

"You may call your next witness," the judge said to Mr. Pearce.

"I call President Thomas Edmonds to the stand."

The crowd whispered as the president entered through the back doors. Harmon was interested to hear what he had to say. Thomas made his way into the witness box.

Mr. Pearce approached the witness. "Would you please state your name and occupation?"

Thomas rested his hands on the chair's arm rests and answered, "My name is Thomas Edmonds. I'm the President of Baltia."

"Do you know Michael Soros?" Mr. Pearce asked, pointing to Michael in the second row.

Thomas looked out into the audience. "Yes."

Mr. Pearce turned to face the audience. "What did he tell you?"

Thomas stared straight at Harmon and replied, "He told me two assassins were planning to kill me."

Harmon was surprised Thomas had known about his involvement for so many months and never said anything to him. All this had gone on behind his back. He wondered why Thomas had kept this a secret for so long. He had noticed Thomas studying him from time to time, and now he knew why.

"Did he say anything else?" Mr. Pearce turned to face Thomas.

"He told me Harmon Sinclair had hired these men," said Thomas, still staring at Harmon.

Harmon wouldn't give Thomas the pleasure of seeing him squirm. He stared back at Thomas, challenging him to look away first.

"I see," said Mr. Pearce. "What did you do with this information?"

Thomas nodded his head at some men standing by the side door. "I informed my guards of the assassination, but I kept the fact Mr. Sinclair had ordered it a secret."

Mr. Pearce looked at him. "Why?"

"I was shocked by the information," admitted Thomas. He crossed his arms across his chest. "I didn't want to believe it was true, so I decided to watch Mr. Sinclair instead."

Mr. Pearce pointed at Harmon. "Did he give himself away?"

Thomas shook his head. "No, he did not."

Mr. Pearce walked over to his briefcase and pulled out a legal pad. He played with the pages until he found the right piece. "What happened the night of Monday, November sixth?"

"I went for my usual run in the park," explained Thomas. "As I reached the forest, I felt a sting in my neck, and I lost consciousness. I woke up with my guards around me."

"Thank you, President Edmonds. No more questions," said Mr. Pearce.

"Your witness," the judge addressed Mr. Moss.

Mr. Moss rose from his chair. "President Edmonds, I respect and honour you as our president, but you'll agree my client deserves a defence?"

Thomas breathed deeply. "Yes, I understand your position."

Mr. Moss walked around his table and stood before Thomas. "Do you know of any reason why my client would want to kill you?"

Thomas shrugged. "I have no idea."

Mr. Moss held up his hands. "Has he ever given you any indication he wanted to kill you?"

"No, he has not." Thomas crossed his legs.

"Wouldn't you think, perhaps, this Mr. Soros mistook my client for someone else?" asked Mr. Moss.

Thomas shook his head. "No. I trust his word."

Mr. Moss continued, "But he had been drinking, and maybe he couldn't hear too well over the noise in the bar?"

"I believe him." Thomas remained perfectly still.

Mr. Moss wouldn't give up. "Wouldn't you agree that possibly Mr. Soros has the wrong man?"

"No," Thomas said, sitting up straight. "He identified Harmon Sinclair as the man who hired the assassins."

Mr. Moss waved a blank piece of paper in front of Thomas. "I understand the assassins revealed nothing?"

"That's correct." Thomas looked embarrassed his guards had not succeeded in finding the truth from the assassins.

"They didn't tell you who hired them?" Mr. Moss pushed the point.

Thomas appeared uncomfortable as he moved around in his chair. "No, they didn't."

Noticing Thomas's body language, Mr. Moss asked, "So isn't it possible my client wasn't the culprit?"

"Of course it's possible, but I'm sure Mr. Soros has the right man." Thomas tried to stare down Mr. Moss, but he wouldn't comply.

Harmon covered a laugh with a hand to his mouth. He wouldn't allow Thomas to see him smile.

Mr. Moss turned towards the judge. "No more questions, Your Honour."

"Mr. President, you are free to leave the stand," the judge directed.

Thomas stood up, glared at Harmon, and then smiled at the crowd. He glided down the aisle to find a seat.

"Your next witness, Mr. Pearce," said the judge.

Mr. Pearce faced the judge. "Our last witness is Mr. Derrick Upton."

The guard in the corner said, "Would Derrick Upton please come forward?"

Mr. Upton rose from his seat in the fourth row and walked up the aisle to the witness box. His face looked like it was chiselled out of stone; no emotion played on it. His steely blue eyes glared at Harmon.

As soon as the man sat down in the witness box, Mr. Pearce said, "Please state your name and occupation."

"My name is Derrick Upton. I'm the president's head bodyguard."

Mr. Pearce walked over to him. "What do you know about the assassination?"

Only moving his lips, Mr. Upton answered, "The president informed me about the two assassins."

"What did you do with this information?" asked the prosecutor.

"We located the assassins in an old hotel on the outskirts of town. We kept them under surveillance then followed them the night of the sixth."

Harmon didn't know this. The assassins never had a chance. Thomas had always been safe and the assassination had no hope of success. This information frustrated him.

"Very good," said Mr. Pearce. "What happened next?"

Mr. Upton replied, "We followed the men to the park and watched their movements."

Mr. Pearce encouraged the witness to continue. "What did they do?"

"They shot the president with a tranquillizer gun, grabbed him, and then stuffed him into the trunk of their car. We were hiding nearby. We overpowered them, handcuffed them, and placed them in a secure vehicle."

"Very good," Mr. Pearce repeated. He referred to a paper on his table. "You interrogated these assassins?"

Mr. Upton slowly moved his head up and down. "Yes, we did."

"Did they give away any information?"

"No, they did not."

"No more questions," concluded Mr. Pearce.

"Your witness, Mr. Moss," the judge directed.

Mr. Moss remained seated in his chair beside Harmon. For a few moments, he shuffled through some papers in his briefcase before finally extracting a thick notepad.

The judge appeared irritated. "Mr. Moss, do you have any questions for this man?"

Mr. Moss glanced from Harmon to the judge. "No questions."

"Mr. Upton, you are excused," said the judge.

The stoic guard returned to the audience. Harmon followed him with his eyes. As he sat down, the man beside Upton whispered a few words in his ear, and Upton laughed. Harmon was surprised to see emotion on his stone face.

Mr. Pearce stood up. "No more witnesses, Your Honour."

The judge nodded his head at Mr. Pearce then said, "Does the defence wish to bring forward any witnesses?"

"No, Your Honour," answered Mr. Moss. "We have no witnesses."

Harmon grabbed his lawyer's arm and whispered, "Put me on the stand."

"No way," Mr. Moss whispered back.

Harmon grumbled in his chair. Mr. Moss had spoken to him about bringing someone to testify on his behalf, but Harmon couldn't think of anyone who would help his case.

The judge made a few notes and then said, "Mr. Pearce, would you like to give your closing summation?"

"Yes, thank you, Your Honour," said Mr. Pearce. He rose from his chair and came to stand before the judge. He turned his head and glared at Harmon.

"Your Honour, I have unequivocally proven that the defendant, Mr. Harmon Sinclair, is guilty of treason. Not only did he hire the assassins to kill the president, he planned the assassination. But the assassination was discovered and our president lives. The defendant should be charged with treason and hanged by the neck until he is dead." Mr. Pearce returned to his chair.

Harmon automatically put his hand to his throat and held it there. He coughed until Mr. Moss poured him a glass of water. Everyone in the courtroom watched Harmon drink.

"Mr. Moss," said the judge. "Would you please give your closing remarks?"

"Thank you, Your Honour," replied Mr. Moss. He rose from his chair but did not move from behind the table.

"My client is an innocent man. The witness, Mr. Soros, was too drunk to recognize him. In addition, the bar was crowded and noisy. He was unable to understand any of the assassins' conversation. I ask, Your Honour, that you find my client not guilty and set him free."

After that statement, the audience jumped to their feet and shouted angry comments. The judge had to hit his gavel to silence the crowd. After a few minutes, the courtroom went quiet, waiting expectantly for the judge to speak.

"Thank you. I will retire to my chambers to deliberate on this case." The judge looked down at his calendar. "I will give my verdict in two days' time on Wednesday at nine o'clock in the morning."

The guard spoke, "Everyone, please rise."

Everyone in the courtroom stood while the judge rose from his chair, and they watched him leave the courtroom.

Harmon felt like putting his arms on the table and weeping, but he had to stay strong. He didn't want to give anyone the satisfaction of seeing him defeated. He shook Mr. Moss's hand and turned to head out of the courtroom. A guard appeared at his side, grabbed him by the arm, and guided him into a white van waiting by the back door.

Looking out the window, Harmon tried to memorize the view. He would remain in his prison cell until the execution. The execution. Those words terrified him.

Back in his cell, Harmon crawled into bed. The prosecutor had done a good job, and he was sure the judge would find him guilty and sentence him to death. He wondered if anyone would care.

Chapter Twenty-Seven

On Wednesday morning, Judge Russell Martin pronounced Harmon guilty of treason. As the words were spoken, the whole audience inhaled deeply. When the judge sentenced him to death by hanging, the packed courtroom cheered.

The whole time, Harmon had kept his head down. His pale face showed no emotion. His worst nightmare had come true. Mr. Moss put his arm around his shoulders and spoke a few consoling words, but nothing could help him now. He rested his head in his hands.

Mr. Moss shook him. "Don't let them see you like this. Sit up. You mustn't show weakness."

Harmon pulled back his shoulders and sat up straight. He raised his hands, grabbed a tissue, and wiped the tears from his eyes. He whispered, "I'm okay."

Mr. Moss was right. Harmon couldn't go to his death downcast. He must gather his courage and show confidence. He shouldn't let the people get to him, but they were so annoying. Why did they have to make so much noise? Was he really hated that much?

Harmon reached for his glass of water and drank it down. He wiped his face with his handkerchief and then tucked it into his breast pocket. Once he recovered his composure, he rose from his chair. A guard arrived at his side to return him to his prison cell.

The crowd screamed insults as Harmon was led from the courtroom. Harmon couldn't wait to get out of there. He was glad when the police van door shut but realized it was the last time he would see the outside world.

The prison van only had one window in the back, and Harmon watched the scenery pass by. He said goodbye to every tree, building, and person they left behind. He gazed up into the clear, blue sky and let the sun shine on his face.

The guards in the front seat carried on a conversation about last night's soccer game. Taking breaks from looking out the window, Harmon listened to the guards from time to time, but it wasn't a topic that interested him. The guard in the back of the van with him said nothing but made him feel uncomfortable because of the way he stared at him. Was he worried he would escape? He suppressed a laugh.

Harmon turned his eyes away from the guard. *Fuck him. If he wants to stare, then let him stare.*

He continued to gaze out the back window. Soon the walls of the prison came into view and he knew his journey was over. He felt his knees go weak. Stomping his feet, he tried to bring feeling back into his legs.

His hanging would take place at ten o'clock that night. It was ironic he would be killed on the same gallows he had built for Michael Soros. That man had destroyed his life. Harmon was angry and frustrated that, like Thomas's assassination, Michael's execution was also a failure.

At nine o'clock, he was shown into the prison meeting room. His heart sank when he saw his parents sitting in the cold, stark room. They appeared years older since they had last met, and this would be the last time they would be together.

His mother jumped up from her chair and rushed around the table to stand before her son. She was a little woman, but she stretched her small frame up to reach his face and give him a kiss on the cheek. She then wrapped her arms around him and gave him a heartbreaking hug.

His father remained in his metal chair with anguish on his once-noble face. His sadness was evident, making his wrinkles stand out even more. His hands lay stiffly in his lap, and his back was hunched over. When he looked at Harmon, a tear dropped from his right eye.

Harmon felt totally responsible for his parents' situation; it was all his fault and he would pay with his life. There was nothing he could do to lighten their load. They were simple country folk who had no aspirations in life but to sell their produce. Now, they were associated with a traitor.

Harmon let go of his mother and helped her sit down. "I'm sorry for everything."

His parents seemed preoccupied. They shuffled in their chairs, keeping their attention away from their son.

After a few difficult moments, his father said, "Why did you do it?"

Harmon's mother played with the handkerchief in her hands. She couldn't look her son in the eye.

"I screwed up." Harmon stared at his parents, but they wouldn't look up.

Harmon's father finally raised his head. "No one buys from our vegetable stand anymore."

"I'm sorry," Harmon apologized.

"The farmers have stopped providing us with their produce," added his mother.

"I'm sorry."

"We don't know how we're going to survive," Harmon's mother cried.

"Sell my house and everything in it," instructed Harmon. "That should provide you with enough money."

"Thank you," said Harmon's mother.

Harmon wiggled in his chair. He felt uncomfortable but had to ask one question. "Will you stay until the end?"

Harmon's parents glanced at each other but said nothing. After a couple of minutes, his father whispered, "We'll stay."

Leaving his chair, Harmon moved around the table to hug his parents. His mother stood up and surrounded him with her arms, but his father stayed in his chair. He put out his hand, which Harmon shook, but that was the only physical gesture from him. Harmon knew he was truly ashamed of him, making him feel even worse.

Harmon's father pulled his wife off their son and guided her out of the room. At the threshold, he said, "You have ruined us."

Harmon had nothing left to say. When the door closed, his head fell onto the table with a clunk and he wept. He could no longer hold onto his emotions.

Suddenly, a guard came into the room. Harmon pulled himself together and dried his eyes. He didn't want the guard to see him crying.

"You have another visitor," advised the guard.

Harmon wondered who it could be. Then Thomas entered the prison room. A small smile played on his glowing face.

"What do you want?" Harmon growled.

Thomas moved to the other chair and sat down. He adjusted his suit jacket and glared at Harmon. "Why did you do it?"

Harmon had no strength left. His parents' visit had crushed him. He shook his head and answered, "It doesn't matter now."

"Yes, it does. Answer me!" Thomas ordered as he moved to stand directly in front of Harmon.

Harmon gazed up at Thomas and said nothing.

"C'mon now, Harmon. You owe me that much," pressed Thomas.

Harmon slowly enunciated each word. "I owe you nothing,"

"What's the big deal? You're going to die in thirty minutes," Thomas said, glancing at his wrist watch. "Tell me."

Exasperated, Harmon gave in. "Oh, fuck it. I wanted to be president."

Thomas shook his head. "What a waste."

Harmon snickered. "By the way," his face broke out into a big smile. "Leah was a good fuck."

Thomas spat, "What are you talking about?"

Harmon put his hands on his hips and thrust out his chest. "I was fucking Leah for the last two years."

Harmon felt a fist in his face. Thomas knocked him to the ground. Harmon shook his head as he watched Thomas march out of the room. He deserved that, but he was glad to finally tell Thomas about the affair.

After Thomas left, a guard came and steered him towards his cell. He would be alone with his thoughts until the time for the execution. But he didn't want to think. He had been thinking too hard all his life and it had only put him in trouble.

A guard came into Harmon's cell with his dinner. He was asked earlier what he wanted for his last meal. He chose grilled salmon with asparagus and scalloped potatoes. When the meal arrived, he accepted the tray, squatted on the bed, and put the tray on his lap.

He chewed his dinner as slowly as possible in order to enjoy every flavour. He rolled the salmon around in his mouth and let his tongue savour it. He ate the asparagus doused with butter, and the butter dripped off his chin. He wiped his mouth with a napkin, but he licked the butter off his fingers.

The potatoes were perfectly prepared. The sprinkling of dill and parsley elevated the dish. Using his fork, he cut each potato slice in half and then placed one of the halves on his tongue. He allowed the potato to melt in his mouth.

For dessert, he received a large piece of lemon cake. His favourite. He chewed it in small bites to make it last. The icing had a perfect lemony taste, causing his taste buds to zing.

His lawyer had left him with a pack of cigarettes. He retrieved one after his meal and lit it. He inhaled the smoke and allowed it to flow down his throat and into his lungs. Once he felt the smoke move through his body, he exhaled slowly. The smoke made the meal feel better in his stomach. He was sufficiently satisfied.

A few minutes before ten o'clock, a guard arrived to take him to his execution. They strolled through the prison to the centre yard where the gallows were located. He knew it was well-built since he had ordered its construction. It looked ominous from his position on the ground.

As he raised his head, he observed people standing at the windows in the upper rooms. There they would have an unobstructed view of the hanging. He couldn't recognize anyone, which was just as well. Harmon didn't want to know who was standing there.

He was guided to a set of stairs. The guard placed a hand on his back as he stepped up to the platform. He was then positioned over the trap door. Another guard was there with a black hood, which was placed over his head. He felt a rope looped around his neck. It was pulled tight.

This is it. Goodbye, Leah. Goodbye, Baltia. Goodbye, world.

The guard hit a button, and the trap door opened. Harmon fell through, breaking his neck. After a few minutes, the guard lowered the rope, and Harmon dropped onto the ground where a doctor checked him. The doctor stood up and nodded his head. Harmon was dead. The crowd cheered.

Chapter Twenty-Eight

Thomas's cell phone, lying on the bedside table, rang, waking both Thomas and Katie. After Thomas rubbed the sleep out of his eyes, he picked up the clock. It read half past four. Yawning, he answered the phone.

"Sorry to bother you, sir. This is chief firefighter, Allan Cerns, speaking. There has been a massive blaze in town."

"Where?" Thomas was now fully awake.

"On Burdock Lane, near Sanders Road," answered the chief.

Thomas rubbed his finger on his chin. "I think I know that area. It's a large townhouse complex?"

"Yes, sir. The fire started in the middle townhouse, and then quickly spread, taking down the whole row."

Thomas moved the phone from his right ear to his left. "How many homes does that entail?"

"Ten, sir," answered the chief.

Thomas breathed deeply. "Ten homes?"

"Yes, sir."

"Did you get everyone out? Any injuries?" Thomas asked as he placed his hand over his heart.

"Yes. Everyone is accounted for, and there were no serious injuries."

Thomas slowly exhaled, relieved no one had died. "Where are the inhabitants now?"

"They're safe in a city bus," replied the chief.

Katie placed a hand on Thomas's arm. Her eyebrows were raised, and she mouthed, "What?"

Thomas asked the chief to hold for a second while he passed on the news to his wife. After he pressed the mute button, he filled her in with everything the chief had said.

"That's horrible," murmured Katie. "We have to find a place for those families."

Thomas returned to the phone. "Chief, let me talk to some people. We'll find somewhere for them to go."

"Yes, sir. I'll tell them."

Katie whispered, "The cause?"

Thomas nodded his head, then asked the chief, "Do you know the cause of the fire?"

"Not yet," answered the chief. "The buildings are still too hot to enter."

"We'll be there in fifteen minutes," Thomas said, and then he hung up.

Sitting up in bed, Katie asked, "Can I go with you?"

"Of course." Thomas gave his wife a quick kiss, and then he rolled off the bed.

The couple dressed and then headed for the garage. They jumped into Thomas's blue Lexus and made their way to the townhouses on Burdock Lane.

On the way, Thomas said, "Take my phone."

Katie pulled his cell out of his jacket pocket.

"Please call my secretary."

"Jane Wood?"

"Yes. Ask her to call around to hotels in the area to see if they could provide rooms for the homeless families," instructed Thomas.

Katie searched through his contacts until she found Jane's number. When Jane answered her call,

Katie apologized for waking her so early, but then explained the situation to her.

"I'll call you right back, Mrs. Edmonds," replied Jane.

After Katie relayed this to her husband, she squirmed in her seat and her face contorted, implying some kind of pain.

"You okay?" he said.

Katie eked out a smile and said, "Just a little morning sickness."

"Do you need me to stop anywhere?"

"No, dear, thanks. I'm fine. This will pass."

When they arrived at Burdock Lane, they were shocked to see the number of fire trucks and police vehicles in the area. They parked the car and had to walk the last block to reach the scene.

They were headed towards a group of firefighters when Fire Chief Cerns approached them. "Hello, Mr. President. I'm Chief Cerns."

After the men shook hands, the chief tipped his hat to Katie.

"Is the fire under control?" Thomas asked, waving his hand at the buildings in ruin.

"Yes, sir. It started in unit eight," he said, pointing to the middle house.

"Were all the units destroyed?" Thomas frowned at the mess in front of him.

"Yes," the chief said, nodding his head. "All ten."

Katie put a hand on Chief Cerns's arm. "Is that ten families out of their homes?"

"Yes, Mrs. Edmonds," replied the chief. "We put them in that bus over there."

Katie looked to where he was pointing and saw a large yellow city bus full of people. She immediately headed in that direction, but she had to manoeuvre around a couple of reporters.

She recognized one and said to her, "Alice? Alice Mann is it?"

Alice stepped forward. "Yes, ma'am. Thank you for remembering me."

Katie gave her a wide smile. "Can I borrow you and your pad and paper?"

"Sure, Mrs. Edmonds," Alice replied, turning to a fresh page. "What can I do for you?"

"Follow me." Katie pointed to the city bus standing by the curb.

Upon reaching the bus, Katie knocked on the front door. It was immediately opened by a woman wearing a black jacket with the word *Paramedic* written in yellow on it.

"How's everyone?" Katie asked while climbing the stairs into the bus.

"A few people with minor smoke inhalation," said the paramedic. "We have them on oxygen."

Katie looked around the bus. "They are all accounted for?"

"Yes, ma'am," said the paramedic as she juggled a few pieces of equipment in her hands. "Luckily, the fire alarms sounded in time for everyone to get out."

"That's wonderful news," sighed Katie. She walked down the row of fire victims.

"Are you okay?" Katie asked a couple with two young children. They were covered in blankets.

"We're fine, but we lost everything," the husband said. "What are we going to do now?"

Katie put her hand on his arm and looked into his sad, brown eyes. "We are arranging a hotel. We'll deal with one thing at a time. Is there anything you need at this moment?"

The man turned to his wife. She said, "The children could use some juice."

Katie smiled at the children and patted the head of the one closest to her. "As soon as we find a hotel, we'll arrange for food and drinks."

She straightened her back, putting a hand on her hip. Then she said to Alice, "Write that down, please."

Alice made a note that a meal was necessary.

"Some clothes would be nice," said the man as he pulled aside his blanket to reveal he was only wearing pajamas.

Katie glanced around the bus and noticed all the survivors were dressed in their night clothes. "Alice, would you please ask everyone their clothes' size? We'll have to find them something to wear."

"Yes, Mrs. Edmonds," replied Alice, who then talked to all the families, making a note of everything.

A few rows away, Katie noticed a little girl crying in her mother's arms. She walked over to the girl and asked, "What's the matter, my dear?"

Her mother answered for her, "Emma lost her favourite doll in the fire."

"I'm so sorry, Emma. What kind of doll was it?"

Emma dried her eyes and whispered, "Elsa."

"Do you mean the Elsa doll from the movie *Frozen*?"

Emma nodded her head.

"We'll get you another one. I promise," said Katie.

Emma's mother smiled at Katie while hugging her daughter. Emma attempted a smile.

"Excuse me, Mrs. Edmonds," said a man in the next row.

Katie moved over to him and asked, "Is there anything I can do for you?"

"Yes, please," replied Bill. "We all lost our cell phones. We need to contact our families to let them know we're safe."

Katie dug into her purse and retrieved her cell phone. "Take mine."

"Thank you, but we cannot take your phone."

"Of course you can," assured Katie. "Pass it around. Return it when everyone has made their calls."

"Thank you," Bill said as he gratefully accepted the phone. He turned it on and called his parents.

Alice made her way back to Katie who asked her to write down an Elsa doll for Emma.

"Some of the other children are asking for things," Alice said, while making a note about the doll.

"Please write it all down," instructed Katie. She then turned to the paramedics at the front of the bus. "You all look like you could use a strong cup of coffee."

The three paramedics smiled. The one who had opened the door for her said, "Thank you, Mrs. Edmonds. That sounds good about now."

"There's a Starbucks down the street. Here, take this," Katie said holding out a Starbucks card. "Order whatever you want."

"Thank you, Mrs. Edmonds," said one of the paramedics.

"I'd like to speak with my husband now," Katie said to Alice as she walked off the bus. They made their way over to where her husband stood with the fire chief and a few other men.

Katie overheard one man say, "All ten homes are a complete loss."

"In a few moments, the fire marshal will test unit eight to see if he can go in," said the fire chief.

Katie followed the men's eyes over to a man in a green jacket holding some equipment. He was talking to a man beside him while pointing to unit eight.

Katie slid over to Thomas's side and tugged on his arm. "I've talked to the families. We've made notes of everything they need. Has a hotel been arranged?"

"Yes," said Thomas. "The Fairfield has agreed to take all ten families."

"That's great. It's a nice place. I'd like to call ahead and ask them to prepare some food and drinks," said Katie.

"Here, take my phone. The number is there."

Thomas passed Katie his cell phone, and she called the hotel to arrange a few things. After she hung up, she said to Thomas, "I'm going with the families to the hotel. I want to make sure they get everything they need."

"Fine, dear. Thanks. I'm going to stay here," Thomas said while recognizing a man who had just walked up to the group. "The man representing the condo corporation is here, and I'd like to talk to him."

"Okay. I'll see you later," Katie said as she reached up to kiss him on the cheek.

Katie joined the bus as it travelled to the Fairfield Hotel. Once they arrived, she spoke to the manager who assured her the families would receive everything they needed.

Turning to Alice, she asked, "Care to join me in a shopping spree?"

"Sure. Sounds like fun," said Alice.

The two women spent the morning shopping, and only returned to the hotel when they had bought enough clothes for the families and some toys for the children.

After passing everything out, Katie asked Alice, "Could you help me get the word out that we need donations for the families?"

"Would you like to collaborate on an article for the paper?" asked Alice, holding up her pen.

"Yes, please." Katie gave Alice one of her beaming smiles. "Begin the article with a description of the fire and what occurred. Then ask everyone to go through their homes and put aside anything not needed. Have them bring it all to the Grand River Community Centre."

"Okay," said Alice. "I've got that. Anything else?"

Katie nodded. "I'll be at the Centre the morning the article runs to receive the items personally."

"That will get people out," said Alice, writing it down. "Everyone loves to see you."

"Thank you, Alice. Can you get this in tomorrow's paper?"

"Yes," answered Alice. "The deadline is ten o'clock. I have time to get it in, and I'll try for the front page."

"That's great." Katie reached over and hugged Alice.

Then the women parted ways. Alice headed for the newspaper office to finish the article, and Katie caught a taxi home. She found Thomas in his study, working on his computer.

"Hello, my dear," Thomas greeted her. He closed the laptop screen, rose from his chair, and placed his arms around his wife.

"I'm so glad to be home," said Katie. She enjoyed her husband's tight hug and held onto him for a few minutes.

"Are all the families settled?" Thomas asked.

"Yes, they have everything for now, but they need a lot of help."

"Any ideas?"

"We should ask all the construction workers and carpenters in the city to help rebuild their homes," Katie suggested.

"Yes," Thomas said as he rubbed his chin with his hand. "We could do that. I shall declare a disaster situation and have everyone take a week's break from their jobs so they can concentrate on rebuilding the townhouses."

"And I think we should have a big party," said Katie. "Everyone has been through so much in the last few weeks. I can get the word out when everyone comes to the community centre to drop off their donations."

"Good idea," Thomas agreed. He grabbed his phone and called his staff to put everything together. He then turned to Katie and asked, "Have you eaten anything today?"

Katie thought about it. "You know, I haven't eaten much."

"Let's have some dinner and an early night. We have much to prepare."

The couple walked hand-in-hand to the dining room where their servants laid out a delicious meal of roast chicken, potatoes, and salad. Once they had eaten their fill, they made their way to their bedroom. Thomas was pleased Katie was interested in making love. They fell asleep in each other's arms.

Chapter Twenty-Nine

While the townhouses were being assessed, the rest of the city's citizens gathered at the Grand River Community Centre. Katie greeted each one personally and accepted the many bags full of personal effects for the families who had lost everything in the fire.

Katie was thrilled to see so many people coming out to support the families. Everyone had done their part, and soon they had plenty of clothes, toys, and kitchen necessities. Some companies even got on board and provided appliances, furniture, and computers.

All ten families helped sort what was brought in, and they appreciated the donations. Katie was happy to see all of them finally smiling. Even the children felt the love from their neighbours.

By ten o'clock, Katie noticed the centre's auditorium was crowded with people. She knew everyone had waited around to hear her speech. She felt it was important to put her stamp on the country as the first lady, beginning with a yearly traditional holiday.

When the time was right, Katie climbed the few stairs to a small stage at the head of the auditorium. A narrow podium and microphone had been set up for her.

"Welcome, everyone," Katie said into the microphone.

The gathered people ended their conversations, and they turned to face the stage.

"We have stood together to support the fire victims so let's celebrate together," said Katie. "Tonight, we'll hold a grand gala."

"What do we call this gala?" shouted someone in the audience.

Kate gave everyone a brilliant smile. "It shall be named 'Purim' for the *pur*, or dice, Harmon rolled to determine the decree date of Michael Soros's execution."

"The man who saved our president?" asked a member of the audience.

"Yes," answered Katie. "Harmon's victimization of Michael has caused him much anxiety and stress. We should honour Michael and his triumph over the wicked Harmon."

The crowd cheered.

Katie continued, "At the party, we'll retell the story of Michael and Harmon and their involvement in the assassination. Whenever someone speaks Harmon's name, I want everyone to scream and shout, making a lot of noise blotting out his name."

Everyone laughed and nodded their heads.

Looking about the auditorium, Katie could tell everyone was pleased with her suggestions, so she continued. "We'll make it a royal masquerade ball. Find clothes and costumes that imitate royalty. I want everyone to feel important."

The crowd puffed out their chests upon hearing those words, and they patted each other on the back.

"We should emulate the traditional royal court. I wish everyone to leave our modern times behind us for a short while and enjoy a past tradition. Leave your cell phones and all your worries at home. Let's have fun!"

Everyone applauded.

When it quieted down, Katie said, "We'll spend the day fasting and praying to remind us of life's struggles. I would like everyone to pass amongst each other a package of pastry and fruit. Women give to women and men give to men. Have the children deliver the packages."

"Done," shouted the crowd.

"At sundown, we'll come together at the presidential palace ballroom and enjoy the festivities. Everyone should bring three half-Euro coins to be donated to the poor families who lost everything in the fire."

"We will," some people shouted.

"Now, go home. We'll meet again at sundown."

Everyone felt the need to hug whoever was close. Then they all went home to prepare the packages and to find a suitable costume for an old-fashioned royal court. It was a joyful and celebratory atmosphere.

Chapter Thirty

The butler knocked at the door of the master bedroom. Thomas opened it. "What is it, Arthur?"

"I'm sorry to bother you, sir," Arthur said. "But there's a baker in the kitchen who'd like to speak with your wife."

"Thank you. I'll tell her."

Thomas closed the door and turned to see his lovely wife dressed in a bright green dress with a sunshine-yellow sash. He smiled as she placed a crown of sapphires on her head, matching her dress. She looked every inch a queen.

"You are needed in the kitchen, my queen," Thomas whispered. She took his breath away.

"Thank you, my king." Katie glided across the floor and kissed him. He had dressed as a king in royal purple robes. A crown of diamonds shone from his head.

Thomas took his wife in his arms and hugged her as tightly as he could. Then he reached down and patted her stomach. Since she wore a full-skirted dress, her small baby bump remained unseen.

He brushed some hair off her face and kissed her lips. "I'm very proud of you."

Katie smiled. "Thank you."

The couple kissed again. Katie then pulled herself away from Thomas with a heavy sigh and left the bedroom. She made her way down to the kitchen. As she passed her staff, she was thrilled to see them dressed in costumes of kings and queens. It was their night to feel like royalty.

When she entered the kitchen, she noticed Ted Merch, the baker, holding a large metal tray. Ted's bakery was a favourite of hers because he made the best butter tarts in the country.

The baker nodded at Katie. "Ma'am, I've prepared a special pastry for tonight's celebration."

He held up the tray for Katie to see what he had made. On it were three-cornered pastries loaded with a poppy seed filling. They smelled sweet and delicious.

Katie picked one up and took a bite. She smiled at Ted. "Wonderful. What do you call them?"

"Harmontashen," said Ted.

"Harmontashen? What does that mean?"

"It means *Harmon's ears*. He never listened to us by closing his ears to us."

"That's the meaning behind the pastries?" Katie asked as she had another bite.

Ted put the tray down on the kitchen counter and waved his hand over them. "I made these to celebrate the weakening of Harmon and commemorating his downfall."

"Marvelous," praised Katie after she had swallowed the last piece. "We shall serve these tonight. Thank you."

Arthur entered the kitchen. "Excuse me, ma'am, but there's a toymaker at the front door who would like to speak with you."

"Thank you, Arthur. I'll meet with him immediately."

Katie and Arthur moved out of the kitchen though Arthur walked a step behind her. When they reached the foyer, they found the toymaker standing on the front porch with a big brown box in his arms.

"How can I help you?" asked Katie.

"I had a wonderful idea. Since I have all these noisemakers in stock, I thought we could shake, blow, and rattle them whenever Harmon's name is mentioned when we retell the story of Harmon and Michael tonight."

"That's a great idea," agreed Katie. "Bring them to the party, and we'll hand them out at the door."

"My pleasure," said the toymaker. He left Katie and returned to his shop to gather together all the whistles, cow bells, and horns in his possession.

The president's staff worked hard to decorate the presidential ballroom. No expense was spared. They covered the walls with yellow and white silk curtains. They were so delicate, even the lightest breeze made them come alive. And, as was the custom, the room was filled with vases of white and yellow flowers. They gave off a sweet scent, which everyone enjoyed.

Suits of shining metal armor stood around the ballroom, as well as large wooden chairs covered with red sheets, each one looking like a throne. The staff raided a garden centre and placed small potted trees near the walls. They arranged golden balls around their branches, making them seem like golden fruit trees.

The Baltians came together at sundown and marveled at the exquisite ballroom. After passing through the main door, each person dropped three half-coins into a metal box and received a noisemaker. Once they were told the reason for the toy, the people approved its purpose.

Each citizen wore a royal costume, and those clothes showed off a profusion of red, purple, yellow, green, and blue, appearing like a bed of wild flowers. Everybody's mood was high, and they looked forward to drinking wine and partying.

It was a grand celebration. The people of Baltia partied the whole night long, drinking and telling the stories of Harmon and Michael, and Michael's deliverance from execution. Whenever Harmon's name was mentioned, everybody made as much noise as possible. They rattled their noisemakers or blew their horns while stamping their feet to obliterate his name. It was a noisy banquet.

When Katie and Thomas appeared, the crowd clapped and cheered for Katie. The noise resounded throughout the room. Katie appeared happy and relaxed, and Thomas was obviously proud of his wife. Their love was clear to everyone because of the way they looked into each other's eyes.

At the party, Katie was honoured. Glasses were raised to her and stories were told. When they chronicled her life, their heartfelt words described her with love, admiration, and heartwarming devotion. They couldn't believe their luck that she was their first lady.

Five months after Purim, Katie gave birth to a son. One year later, she gave birth to another son, and then two years later, she gave birth to twin girls. Thomas was thrilled with a house full of his offspring and such a loving wife.

Katie's fame circled the world. She became known for her strength of character, her kindness, and her gentle intelligence. Her position as first lady was revered by the citizens of Baltia, and she became known as a champion of the people.

Author's Notes

The Book of Esther is the only book in the Bible that doesn't mention God and there are more galas/banquets/parties in the Book of Esther than in any other book in the Bible.

A huge thanks to Sarah Fox and Bethany Jamieson-Mansour. Without them, I would never have completed this novel.

About the Author

Born in Nova Scotia, Patty Lesser grew up in Ontario, Canada. After finishing high school, Patty decided to backpack around the world, returning to Canada periodically. She recently moved to Brantford, Ontario, where she hopes to live for many years.

Patty began writing as a child. She started with poems and later moved on to short stories. A few years ago, she decided to write a novel and now she has just completed her sixth.

You can learn more about Patty on her website, **www.pattylesser.com**